I0663484

Crazy Sexy Love

Rescued Hearts, Book 3

Edie Ramer

Blue Walrus Books

ISBN-13: 978-1-939328-15-1
ISBN-10: 19393281512

Cover design by Laura Morrigan
Editing by Blue Otter Editing
Interior formatting by Author E.M.S.

Printed in the United States of America

Acknowledgments

Thanks to the multi-talented Elle J Rossi, a former professional singer who is now a writer and a cover designer, who took time out of her busy life to give me advice on the music profession. Thanks, too, to editor Amy Knupp from Blue Otter Editing, and to Dale Mayer and Michelle Diener. All three are brilliant and insightful. I'm lucky to know so many brilliant and insightful women.

1

Twenty-three years ago...

The girl's laughter was like the best music Sam Krushing had heard in his four and a half years. Walking down the school bus aisle for his third day of four-year-old kindergarten in Eagleton Grade School, he passed two rows of older girls—probably in sixth grade—to get to the girl with the curly blond hair. He'd seen her in the other 4-K classroom at recess and in the cafeteria, but he'd been busy making friends with boys and girls in his classroom and hadn't paid attention to her.

That was before he'd heard her laugh. If sunlight had a sound, it would be her laughter. It was like sparkles on water, each of them ringing a bell. Sunlight lit up her face and her eyes, too. Hearing her and looking at her, he felt it inside him, like he'd swallowed a piece of the sun.

She was sitting next to a girl, but the seat across the aisle was empty. Instead of heading to the back by his friend Nate, he sat beside a bigger kid, who said, "Hey, that seat is saved."

The bus started with a small jerk, and Sam ignored the bigger kid whose voice was a buzz in his ear. He leaned his head into the aisle.

"I'm Sam," he said. "What's your name?"

The girl was facing away from him, but her friend poked her and pointed at him. The girl swiveled to face him, her yellow curls bouncing.

"I'm Sam," he said again, in case she hadn't heard him the first time. "What's your name?"

"Callie."

"I'm in Mrs. Green's class." He beamed at her. Her voice was almost as wonderful as her laugh.

"I'm in Miss Sanderson's class. I saw you at recess. On the playground."

"Did you see me on the ropes? I got almost all the way across the bars yesterday."

Two girls behind him giggled. The boy next to him groaned. Callie shook her head.

"You can watch me today at recess," he said.

"Okay."

Now everyone around them was giggling, except the boy next to him, who was groaning again. Sam even heard the deeper chuckles of the lady bus driver whose laugh reminded him of his grandma's.

The girl next to Callie was tugging on the short sleeve of her yellow top. Callie smiled at him then turned to her friend, who whispered something to Callie.

Sam sat back, so happy. The way he felt after

riding on the back of his dad's motorcycle, just going down the block and hanging on really tight, though his dad was driving really slow. And then later, when his dad let him bang on the drums at his parent's bar, his dad telling everyone he was going to be a rock star.

This feeling was almost better than playing the drums.

"Dude, you gotta play hard to get," the kid next to him said.

"Leave him be," an older girl behind him said. "I think it's cute."

"Oh yeah?" The kid turned his head. "The little twerp's gotta know that the more you ignore girls, the more they like you."

"Yeah? Who's going to watch you play on the ropes at recess?"

"You are."

The girl snorted, and her friend made a noise like a mouth fart.

Then Callie laughed again, and Sam sat back in his seat, facing forward, smiling at the most wonderful sound in the world. And he was going to see her at recess.

His mom was right. School was the best thing in the world ever.

* * *

"I have a boyfriend." Callie dropped her

backpack on the chair then jumped up and down in their kitchen with all the white cupboards and the white refrigerator and oven, and the light blue walls.

Her mom turned from the stove and looked at her with her eyes big. Like she'd seen a bug on Callie's forehead. "Really? How did that happen?"

"He asked me at recess, and I said yes." Callie smiled, feeling the stretch in her cheeks. "I like him. At recess, he made it all the way across the bars. And he plays drums, too."

"Well...athletic and musical." Her mom bent to look in Callie's face, her eyes the same blue as Callie's, her hair a darker color. "He sounds very impressive."

Callie nodded, not sure what impressive meant, but it sounded like a good word. Her mom used to be a teacher, and she knew a lot of good words. "He's handsome, too. All the girls say so."

"Well, handsome is always a bonus."

Callie nodded again. "But I'm not going to smell his butt."

Her mom straightened, her eyebrows winging up. "What?"

"Like dogs do, Mom." Callie frowned. "Cats, too. I've seen 'em"

"I'm glad you came to that decision. There's a reason we're not dogs and cats. We don't sleep on the floor, do we? Or kneel on the floor and use our tongue to drink water."

Giggling, Callie shook her head. "I know, Mom. But Amy and Danny did it. Amy said it was icky."

"It sounds very icky. You don't show boys the parts you go potty with, okay?"

Her mom had her sick face on, and Callie quickly shook her head. "I won't."

"What's your boyfriend's name?" The sick face went away, her mom smiling again.

Immediately, Callie felt lighter, the tightness in her tummy loosening. "It's Sam. Sam Krushing."

"I know who he is. Brenda and Roger's son." Her mom laughed, and Callie knew she had the prettiest mom in the world. "He really does play the drums. Your dad and I saw him last month at their bar."

"Take me, Mom." Callie jumped up and down. "I want to see him play."

Her mom groaned and sagged into a kitchen table chair. "Oh God. You're too young for this."

"I'm not, Mom, I'm not! I'm in school now."

"You're like a whirlwind. No wonder I'm so tired all the time." She put her elbow on the table, her hand up to hold her head that sagged into it.

"Because of me?" Callie's voice creaked, and she felt herself grow small, her shoulders hunching. "I won't be a wind. I promise. And you don't have to take me to see Sam."

"Oh, baby." Her mom slowly lifted her head then reached out for Callie, who rushed into her embrace. Her mom bent over her, cocooning her in a giant hug while Callie held on to her tightly.

"Sweetie, it's nothing to do with you. It's just that time of the month." She smoothed her hand over Callie's hair then let her go. Callie stepped back as her mom flattened her hands on the table to push up to her feet.

"What time of month is it?" Callie frowned. "I don't like that time."

"Never mind. That's something you won't have to worry about for a long time." She smiled. "And someday soon, your dad and I will take you to watch your boyfriend play his drums."

Callie squealed and clasped her arms around her mom as high as she could, leaning her head against her hip. Still holding on to her, she lifted her head. "I love you, Mom. More than any boy. Ever, ever never."

Her mom laughed, but there was a catch in her voice. "Oh, honey, never say never."

"Okay, I'll never say never." They laughed together, then Callie ran off and her laughter stopped. She felt a small frown pull on her forehead as she wished her mom's time of the month would go away and not come back. Never, never, ever.

2

Twenty-one years ago...

"Everyone get out their readers now." Mr. Waverly's voice boomed like a kettledrum.

Sam's muscles tightened, knowing what was going to happen next.

"Except Sam." His voice seemed even louder now. Like he had an amplifier in his throat. "Sam, time to go to Miss Lemon's room."

Someone at his round table snickered. He didn't look up, though he knew who it was. He could tell everyone in his first grade class by their voice.

If only he could tell words by looking at the letters in a book. But to him it was like looking at squiggles, and none of them made sense.

He knew why. He was stupid.

Not like Callie. She was with the blue readers in her class. Those were the smartest kids. Not him. He wasn't even with the yellow or green readers. He had to go to read with Miss Lemon, all alone, because he couldn't read.

She'd told his mom she wanted to test him.

He didn't know what that meant, but his mom had cried, and his mom never cried, so it wasn't good.

He left the class to go to Miss Lemon's room. As

he passed the last table, Ken Wyler said, "Stupid," in a voice too low for Mrs. Morgan to hear. Timmy Carrabus laughed, and a girl giggled.

Recognizing the giggle, he stiffened. Ariella Aberdeen. Callie's friend. Like Callie, she lived just outside the city. Not like his mom and dad and him. They lived in the middle of Eagleton, on Main Street, above the bar his parents owned. Where his dad played his guitar at night while his mom and Uncle George took care of the bar. Where the music pulsed upstairs through the floors while his cousin Jenny, a junior in high school this year, did her homework or talked on the phone to her friends, letting him play his small drum set in his bedroom with the door closed, banging in time with the music downstairs. Or sometimes the harmonica.

And sometimes his dad and mom let him play the drums downstairs, and people clapped and said he was a genius.

Genius was better than smart.

No one called him stupid at home. Just at school.

He hated school. Hated it. Except for Callie when he got to see her at recess and lunch, and they sat together. Sometimes, though, her friends sat with them. He didn't mind them most of the time, but sometimes they talked about stupid girl stuff. And she and another girl talked about books.

But he and Callie were boyfriend and girlfriend, and his dad said, "If Mama ain't happy, ain't

nobody happy." So he never said anything.
Besides, her girlfriends liked him, too.

They were in the other classroom and didn't
know he was stupid. Neither did Callie. He'd
already told her he wanted to marry her when they
got old enough, and she'd said yes.

But if Ariella told Callie, then Callie wouldn't
want to marry him anymore.

And she wouldn't want to be his girlfriend.

His shoulders drooped. He'd been thinking
about this for a long time. Since the beginning of
the school year. Stepping into the hall, he closed
the door behind him, knowing what he needed to
do.

* * *

Sam's class was on the playground for recess
before Callie's. His plan had been to ignore her, but
she called out his name, and he turned without
thinking.

Callie's face glowed, and she ran to him while he
hung back with his friends. Her jacket flapped
behind her, a brown leaf crumpled under her shoe.

He stepped toward her. She was like the sun,
and he was a weed. He didn't understand words on
paper, but he understood that.

"I guess you're going to play with your
girlfriend," a first grader called, and his other
friends laughed. Out of the corner of Sam's eye, he

saw Ken, the jerk, talking to Ariella, and his stomach hurt.

"Guess what?" Callie hopped up and down three times. "Miss Schuler read my poem aloud in class. She's going to send it to a contest!"

"That's nice." His mom said poems were like songs without music. "What did your poem say?"

"I'll give it to you on the bus going home. You can read it!"

His stomach hurt harder. "You can just tell me now."

"I'll tell you a new one." Her smile widened, filling up half her face, and he could see a gap near the front where a baby tooth was missing. "Girls like pink, boys like to stink." She laughed.

"I know one, too," he said, and opened his mouth again—and stopped. He'd been about to say, *Your eyes are blue, and I love you.* But he couldn't say that.

Instead he had to say something else. Holding back tears, his body so stiff his bones hurt, he started to talk....

* * *

Even after Callie burst into the house, her mom didn't get up from the chair in the living room. It must be that time of the month again, Callie thought. That time of the month was happening a lot.

Callie's throat tightened and her face screwed up and her eyes scrunched to hold back hot tears, only it didn't work.

She hated that time of the month. Hated it and hated it.

But most of all, she hated Sam Krushing.

If he were here, she would kick him.

"Sweetie." Her mom put down her book and lifted her head. "What's wrong?"

Callie ran to her, tears blinding her. Her mom held out her arms to receive her, but when Callie crashed into her and threw her arms around her mom's body, her mom shuddered, as if Callie had hurt her.

Callie just hung on, her head to her mom's rib cage, right under her breast. Other times, when this time of the month happened, her mom needed her. But right now, Callie needed her mom more.

Beneath her ear, she heard the sound of her mom's heartbeat, not quite steady, then Callie's sobs came out. Her mom's arms tightened, and she rocked Callie back and forth.

"What happened, baby? What happened?"

Callie hung on to her mom as tightly as she could. Her heart hurt too much for her to talk.

Her mom made a crooning song, and the tears dripped from Callie's eyes onto her mom's top. Until finally she lifted her head and sniffed.

"It's Sam! He doesn't want to be my boyfriend anymore. He says I'm a girl, and boys don't play with girls."

"Oh, sweetheart. I was afraid this might happen."

"You knew?" She pulled back, feeling as if she'd gotten another stab in her heart.

"I didn't know anything. But you and Sam are so young and—"

"But, Mom, he loved me! He said he wanted to marry me when we grow up."

"Oh, honey, I'm sure he meant it. But things change."

Tears blubbered up inside her eyes again and dribbled down her cheeks. She rubbed them away with the sides of her hands so she could look at her mom. Her dad would come home soon, and he would pick up her mom and twirl her around, and they would laugh, her dad loud and her mom softer, her eyes lit up.

But she wasn't laughing now, and neither was Callie.

She never wanted to laugh again.

She never wanted to fall in love again.

"I hate Sam Krushing. I hate him more than anything in the world."

"I know, sweetie." Her mom pushed up from the chair, and her face twisted. "Let's blow your nose. I know what will make you feel better."

"Mom, nothing is going to make me feel better."

"We'll see." Her mom smiled at her, a small smile. Callie's dad always said she looked beautiful when she smiled, and Callie knew he was telling the truth. When they went places, people would turn to look at her mom.

Dad said she looked like her mom, but Callie didn't think she looked half as pretty.

Right now her mom looked like one of the angels in the picture books.

Instead of making Callie happy, the thought chilled her, drying her tears up so they stopped, but the ones she'd cried already still dribbled down her chin.

She didn't want her mom to be an angel. She wanted her mom to be her mom.

"Come on." Her mom held her hand out to her, and Callie took it. "I'm taking you to a place that I promise will make you happy." With her other hand, she snapped her fingers, making a popping sound. "Just like that."

"Like magic?" Callie asked.

"Just like magic. You'll see."

Callie tightened her grip as they headed to the back door, and her mom grabbed her purse. Her mom was only limping a little, and Callie hoped it meant that time of the month was going away. And she hoped it never came back. Never ever.

"I don't care about Sam already," she said and heard the wobble in her voice. "He's just a stupid boy."

"I know, sweetie." Her mom sighed. "They're all stupid boys."

Callie didn't answer, the tears welling up again. Her throat hurt and so did her heart. She didn't think any magic would make it go away.

* * *

A girl and a woman walked toward the pen in the back, and the puppy jumped up, his nails scrabbling at the metal wires that kept him inside. He whimpered in excitement, pee spraying out.

All his brothers and sisters had gone, one by one, until only he was left.

Why not him? He was cute. They all said that, and then they all picked one of his brothers or sisters to go home with them.

His mom told him they weren't the right humans for him.

Maybe this would be the right humans.

He peed some more.

Then they were there, and he whimpered and he danced and he peed.

The woman who was his mom's human was hurrying toward the pen, but not fast enough. He barked, sending her a sharp message to hurry. *Hurry, hurry, hurry.* He had a human to lick.

Then the woman was there, but she stopped to speak to the other woman instead of opening his pen. Puppy kept his gaze on the girl, and he barked again.

Love me. Take me to your home. I'm your puppy.

*Feed me, pet me, play with me. Do all that, and I'll
love you forever.*

As if she understood, the girl dropped to her
knees in front of the pen. She smelled...wonderful.
Like she belonged to him.

Her fingers poked through the spaces between
the wire links, and the tips of them touched him.
His whole body shook with excitement. He whined,
needing to get out of the pen, needing to get closer
to her. She must have felt the same, because she
pushed her lips between the links. He licked her
mouth. Licked it three times before she pulled
away and laughed. The best sound he'd ever heard.

It made him dance.

"Mommy," the girl said, turning away. "I love
him."

He could feel the mom smiling, but he kept his
gaze on the girl. She was everything to him. He
knew this already. She was the reason none of the
other people had taken him. They were the wrong
people. This girl was the right one. She was *his*
human. She and he belonged together.

The mother's laugh came, softer than the girl's.
"From tears to happiness in two minutes. Puppies
are magic."

The girl bounced up to her feet. "That's his
name! Magic! Can I have him now? Please, Mom?
Please, please, please. I'll take good care of Magic. I
promise."

The mom nodded. "The puppy will be good for

15

you, sweetheart. Maybe he'll be good for all of us." Then her face turned funny, as if it were falling. She came to the pen and crouched, holding out her hand to the pen for him to sniff. "I have a feeling that soon we're going to need a lot of magic."

As Magic pushed his nose out between the wires, he smelled something on the woman's fingers.

Sickness. Something was wrong with her.

Then she pulled back and turned to the other woman, and it was just him and the girl, and Magic wiggled, his tongue out, trying to lick the girl through the wires.

He had a human, and he had a home.
In his excitement, he sprang up and sprang down, and this time he didn't pee. He was happy, happy, happy. And he would never be sad again.

3

Nine years ago...

The graduation party at the Lion's Hall was a cool gig, sponsored by Eagleton Furniture, so Sam's band was getting paid well. Any other night, he would've been happy to play his drums, but any other night he wouldn't have been playing for the group that he should've been graduating with.

He knew now he wasn't stupid, that there was a glitch in his brain. His musical ability more than made up for it, so he figured he got the good end of the learning stick. But when the kids he'd started kindergarten with slow-danced to old standards, his stomach twisted. Especially when he watched Callie in the arms of that jerk, Ken Wyler. Wyler had stopped calling Sam stupid after Sam kicked his butt in second grade. Afterward, Sam's dad hadn't let him play drums in the bar for a month, but it had been worth it. Maybe he couldn't read, but he could fight.

A lot of good it had done him, with Callie swaying in Ken's arms now, her head resting against the jerk's shoulder.

The hell of it was that it was his own fault. All those years ago, he'd lied to her to save his pride.

Once he'd reached his teens, there'd been other girls...but none were Callie. Sometimes since then, he'd be walking in the halls at school and hear her laugh...and his heart would stop for a beat. As if a hand shoved inside his chest and clamped on to it.

Even now, he didn't see what else he could've done. She'd been one of the smartest girls in school, and he'd been the boy who couldn't read, no matter how hard he'd tried every night, staring at the squiggles until his eyes blurred with sleep and tears, trying to make sense of them.

But that was a long time ago, and he needed to get over it. They'd been little kids, four when they'd met and six when he'd broken up with her. It wouldn't have lasted anyway.

And since then, his life had changed. He no longer beat himself up for his learning problem, not since he'd found out it had a name and a lot of people had it. A lot of famous people, too. He could even read now, though it took him twenty times longer than the average person. Maybe thirty times as long as Callie. He and she together would be like mixing fire and rain. Just didn't work. Besides, he had something better than reading. He didn't just have blood pulsing through his veins. He had music, too.

"It's a gift," his dad had said years ago after he'd gone crazy on the drums at the bar during "Hot with Teacher." Getting lost in the music, not thinking of anything except the music and the drumbeats.

After he'd finished, while the bar crowd clapped and hooted, his dad had clasped him in a bear hug and swatted his back. When he'd pulled back, Sam had seen that the eyes of this man who never cried were misted over.

Sam had been eleven.

"Compensation," his mom liked to say. "From the Higher Power."

Sam thought the Higher Power liked playing jokes on people, but as long as he could make music, he was cool with it. He would laugh right along with the Higher Power as he pounded on his drums.

And soon this evening would be over. Done. He could pack up his drums and stop being tortured by the sight of Callie with the asshole.

He played the slow songs on automatic. With the fast songs, he banged the drums as if they were Ken's big head. Fast and hard, so that the other band members turned to look at him, and Rick, his best friend and the lead guitar player, took it as a challenge and started to rock it out like he was Jimmy Hendrix reincarnated, both of them getting dirty looks from Percy, their lead singer and the bass guitar player. Percy was an okay bass player and singer, but nowhere near as good as him and Rick.

The partygoers loved it, though, stopping dancing to watch them. Including Ken and Callie.

Sam kept banging, never out of rhythm, as he stared into Callie's blue eyes. It was like falling into the ocean at the warmest time of the year.

And she stared back at him, as if she were falling into his eyes, too.

He could feel his blood stirring, quickening, foaming like the ocean on a wild, stormy night.

The song changed, but she moved to the edge of the dance floor and watched him along with a pack of other kids. Guys as well as girls. As if they were watching the birth of a panda or something special instead of just him and Rick blasting it out.

Ken bent to say something to Callie, but she shook her head, still staring at Sam. In the corner of his vision, Ken scowled at her then stomped away.

Sam exulted. Yes! Yes, yes, yes! Hell yes!

He pounded the drums harder, stronger, wilder. Empowered by her attention. He was the gorilla showing his mate how high he could swing on a vine. The tiger showing his mate his hunting skills. The eagle who flew high and far for his mate, showing her how strong and fleet he was. Showing her the great genes he could pass on to their eaglets.

And she was watching him as if mesmerized. As if he were the only boy in the place. And he watched her back, as if she were the only girl.

Because she was. Despite the other girls he'd been with, she was the only one for him and had been since he was four years old. Before he'd screwed it up, a little kid who'd thought he was perfect and invincible...until he discovered he wasn't. That's when he'd become convinced he had an insurmountable flaw.

Longing piled up inside him, growing higher by the beat, and so did his intensity. The other band members stopped playing, unable to keep up with his manic rhythm, and he still played, beating the drums for her. In a futile attempt to drown him out, Percy screamed into the mic that it was fun but it was over. Just like school was for them. He yelled out their next date but didn't tell them it would be with another lead guitar player and another drummer. That Sam and Rick were leaving. Percy knew Rick and he were the ones that people came to see.

Sam blasted out one more round of fast moves, feeling the beats through his hands to his soles to the top of his head. They vibrated through his pulse and his heart and in every organ of his body.

This wild song was for Callie, only for her. He was her peacock, and she was his peahen.

Finally it was done, and there was a wild round of clapping and shouts and a few sharp whistles. Exultation whipped through him as Percy took a bow, as if the applause was for him, the douche. Rick stepped up to Sam, slapped him on his back, and laughed.

"You got her attention, kid," he said, though he

was only three months older than him.

Sam ignored him, all his attention on Callie and all of hers on him, making him feel seven feet tall.

He put down his sticks then stepped across the stage and jumped down. All the while, she still stared at him. And in her eyes, he saw the same hurt as when they were six years old, and he'd told her that he couldn't have a girlfriend anymore.

Hurt and pain.

He grew cold then hot. She wasn't mesmerized by him as he'd thought in his self-conceit. It was something more that had kept her watching him. There was desperation in her eyes, as if he were the last man in this place who would save her.

"What happened?" He bent over her. "What the hell happened to you?"

She didn't answer. She just stared at him out of her summer-sky eyes with a storm in the center.

He clasped his long fingers around her upper arms. "Did someone hurt you?" His voice was like hard gravel. If anyone hurt her, they would pay.

Her head shook slowly. "You wouldn't understand."

"Tell me."

"My dog died today."

A pang stabbed through him. He hadn't known she had a dog. And he didn't know why not knowing hurt him, but it did.

He curved his hand over the back of her head, feeling the fineness of her skull beneath her silken hair. "What was her name?"

Kids walked by them and around them. He was aware of their curious gazes, but they were easy to ignore. They didn't matter any more than flies at a picnic. Only Callie mattered.

"Magic. And it's *his* name."

"That's a great name. You want to tell me about him? You have a picture?"

She finally took her gaze from his while she pulled her cell phone out of the tiny purse hanging from her shoulder. While the kids near them laughed and joked, she frowned at the phone and showed him a photo of a brown dog.

"A spaniel?"

"Mmmhmm, cocker." She clicked through to another picture and then another while people strolled around them, as if they were the pillars that held up the building. He ignored their curious stares as he looked at photos of the dog and murmured about Magic's cuteness and the intelligence in his eyes.

Some were of her and the dog at various ages. A few were of her parents. They'd been coming to his parents' bar once or twice a week since he could remember. Not heavy drinkers, but they listened to the music and chatted with friends. This last year, though, her mom had walked in slowly, leaning on a cane. MS, his dad had told him. Multiple Sclerosis.

He'd looked it up on YouTube, carefully and

slowly typing in the letters *MS*. After he'd watched a video, he'd wanted to call Callie up but hadn't. She didn't consider him a friend, and she wouldn't want to know she was on his mind way too much. He'd hurt her when they were kids, and he'd thought she considered him as an enemy and would never forgive him.

But now, after all these years, he was the one she'd turned to in her grief.

As he stared at a photo of her hugging a long-eared, curly-haired dog, he admitted the truth to himself—he'd never forgiven himself.

He'd taken the coward's way out.

He'd been afraid she would reject him, so he'd rejected her first.

A hand on his shoulder caught his attention. He raised his gaze to Rick, a skinny guy with wild dark hair, tattoos, and slashing eyebrows that made his eyes look intense. A tall girl glued to his side smelled of perfume and beer.

"I packed your drums in your van," Rick said. "You leaving soon? I'm driving home with Laura."

"Lorna." The girl's gaze didn't leave Rick's face. "You're so...so..."

He kissed her. "So are you, gorgeous." He waved and gave Sam his we're-getting-lucky grin, then he and Lorna headed for the exit.

Noticing the silence, Sam glanced around and saw there were only a few small groups of partiers left. While they were talking, everyone else had left.

He peered down at Callie. "You have a ride?"

She blinked at him. "I don't..." Frowning, as if she weren't quite sure how she'd ended up talking to him in a fast-emptying hall, she shook her head then turned to scan the room. When she turned back to him, she was sucking in her lower lip.

"You came with Ken?" he asked.

She nodded.

"Good riddance. He's an ass. I'll drive you home."

Her frown didn't leave. He put his arm around her shoulders and tugged her with him. He felt her reluctance. He'd drawn her to him with his wild drumming, sending out a primal message just to her. But now the room was quiet; the echoes of his drumbeats were gone. Silenced. Ashes like her dog.

She let him guide her toward the door, though. He hoped it meant she trusted him to take her home safely. But it was probably just that she needed a ride, and since the asshole was gone, he was it.

Outside it was cool, which was normal June weather in Wisconsin: hot one day, cool the next. Too chilly for the silky, purple dress she wore that skimmed her hips and butt.

"Cold?" he asked, and heard the gruffness in his voice. He wanted her to say yes. He wanted to put his arm around her and warm her with his body heat and his kisses.

This grown-up Callie was making him feel

emotions that the younger Callie hadn't.

He wondered if she'd felt the same way.

"I'm okay." She walked toward his van with him, her head down.

Still, he hoped. She'd come to him tonight in the hall, and she wasn't home yet. Anything could happen.

4

She sat next to him in his van, thinking she should have stayed home tonight. Magic's death was still so recent, two days ago, and she wasn't crazy about Ken. She'd only gone to the party tonight to keep her mom from worrying about her.

But inside, she was grieving, her emotions raw and her heart bleeding.

There was too much sadness in her house. Too much sickness. Too much pretending to be okay when she was hurting inside.

"What if I don't want to go home?" She glanced at Sam and hoped he'd missed the wobble in her voice and the way it had thickened.

"Where do you want to go?" he asked.

She laughed, but it was a cry in her heart. An old wound, never quite healed since she was six, opened up.

Of course, Sam didn't want to drive her around all night. When he'd played the drums tonight, it had felt as if he were playing them just for her. But that was her grief talking. That was because she'd wanted so badly for him to be playing just for her.

"You have plans? You want to drop me off somewhere?" She took a deep breath, told herself she had to be strong. She opened her mouth, but he spoke first.

"If it were up to me," he said, his voice husky, "I'd never drop you off."

Her breath hitched, and she turned to stare at him. They were driving down Main Street. Though it was dark out, light from the streetlamps flickered into the car, giving her surreal glimpses of his face as he stared straight ahead, his square jaw firm and his face tense. His brown hair and eyes blended into the car's black interior, and she felt the emotion pinging off him. As if he were one of his drums, his energy vibrating against the van walls and her skin.

"That's not what you told me twelve years ago," she said.

"Twelve years ago, I was six. A kid."

She switched her gaze to the road ahead, but all her senses focused on him, and she was intensely aware of the boy at her side. No, not a boy. A man now. "So was I. You broke my six-year-old heart."

He didn't reply. They came to the middle of the city when he twisted the wheel and the tires squealed, and she jerked sideways, the seat belt digging into her shoulder through the thin material of her pale purple dress.

She hadn't been paying attention to where they were. *Where* hadn't mattered to her. None of the things that usually mattered to her had mattered. As if she were someone else tonight instead of the cheerful girl who always did well in school and was nice to everyone. Who *had* to be nice. Other girls could get in trouble and be wild. Other girls didn't have sick moms who had good days and bad days...and worse days.

But tonight she was different. The feelings she had crammed down for so long now, buried and locked away, had sprung out. Wide awake. As if Magic's passing had ripped off the old scar tissue, revealing the mass of nerves.

The car squealed into the alley, and she clasped her hands tightly, aware that he was heading into the parking lot of his parents' bar. Aware that he and his parents lived on the floor above it.

The parking lot was full, but he pulled up to the No Parking spot behind the garage and turned the key, the engine shuddering to a stop.

Her heart shuddered, too.

"I'm dyslexic," he said.

"I know." She stared at the tan garage door. Impossible not to know when they went to the same school.

He didn't talk right away. And she sat back, her seat belt still on. His was still on, too.

"I thought you were too good for me," he said.

"I am too good for you."

He laughed, and she heard the hollowness.

"But not because of your dyslexia." She turned her head to him, still held back by the seat belt. "Why didn't you tell me?"

Looking straight ahead, he shrugged. "Back

then, all I knew was that I couldn't read. People were calling me stupid."

"You weren't stupid. I always knew that."

He didn't answer right away, and a muscle jumped in his face, his cheekbone clenching and unclenching.

She raised her hand to his upper arm and felt the tension in his bicep. "*Who* called you stupid?"

"Your date tonight, for one."

"Ken?"

He nodded.

"I *hate* Ken."

He laughed, a surprised burst that stopped quickly. He turned to face her, and she saw the change in his face—the tenderness, the warmth, the openness.

"It was a long time ago."

"I know." She stared at him. "But I never forgot."

His eyes flickered. "Neither did I. You were my first love."

"And you were mine."

"You were hard to beat." His voice grew husky again, but with a different note. One that stirred emotions inside her body. One that made her heart beat louder, her breath come faster. "I never found anyone to match you."

"I know."

"You, too?"

"Not quite. I had Magic."

"Your dog?" He laughed again, low and soft, as if

they'd shared something important, something intimate. "And I had my drums."

They both stared at one another, and more of the pain oozed out of her. It felt as if this were meant to be. She'd gotten Magic because he'd left her. Now Magic had left her, and she had him again.

She released her seat belt and lifted her hand to his shoulder. Beneath the cotton of his black T-shirt, she felt the hardness of his muscle and the heat of his skin. He was hot. As hot as she felt inside.

He closed his eyes, as if he were putting this moment to memory—though maybe that was what she wanted him to do. Then he opened his eyelids and covered her hand with his. She thought he was going to squeeze it, but he pulled it down.

"I'm leaving tomorrow," he said. "I want you, but I need to leave this place. I need to make music."

She stilled, staring into his eyes, and he stared back into hers, unblinking, his face taut, his cheekbones rigid.

"You can make music here."

"I know. I won't even have to get gigs. I could play at my parents' bar whenever I want."

"That's not enough for you." She tried to smile and failed. "Your talent is too big for Eagleton. You need to share it with the world."

Another surprised laugh came from him, and the tension eased from his face and his shoulders, even as he shook his head. "The world will survive without me. I can even survive without my music. I know it's tough, and maybe there's one chance in a few million that I might make it. But I've got to try."

"I know you do." Oddly, she did, feeling his intensity, the primal core of him.

"There's a *need* inside me. I need this the same way a bird needs to fly. I feel that I have to do this...." He exhaled through his nostrils, the sound loud in the car with all the windows closed. "I might never make it, but I've gotta give it my best. Maybe I'm crazy, but I feel there's something *bigger* that I'm supposed to do."

"You'll make the world better with your music."

"Not better. Maybe happier, and just for a few minutes. For those minutes, I can make people forget their troubles. Stop worrying and just feel. That's what music does. Good music."

Sadness returned, even as she smiled. But this was a different sadness. An aching sadness instead of a heartbreaking one. She shifted and put her arm around his shoulder. "You're leaving tomorrow, but you're here now. And so am I."

His breath hissed in, and he jerked away from her.

Now she tensed and twisted to stare at the garage doors on the back of the restaurant. Once again, he was rejecting her, and pain sliced through her.

* * *

The hurt flashing across her face took him back twelve and a half years, to one of the worst days of his life.

She'd said he'd broken her heart that day, but he'd broken his own heart, too. He'd thought he didn't have a choice. He'd thought he wasn't worthy of her.

And he probably wasn't.

But now here she was, sitting next to him.

Was he going to be stupid again?

"We're not little kids anymore." He heard the thickening of his voice. A bass sound that came from deep within him, and he recognized the sound of sex.

She glanced up at him, her eyes wide. Not quite trusting him. Not quite sure what he was going to do. If he was going to hurt her again.

He could see all of this in her face. Maybe he couldn't read words in a book without a struggle, but he could read her eyes that searched his face right back, and he knew her senses were raised like his were. Looking and listening and even smelling for clues. Afraid of being hurt. Afraid of hurting her.

And that was so wrong.

Love shouldn't be about fear.

Neither should sex.

Sex should be good. Fun. Leave you feeling

great. After all, men and women were like any other animals that way: put on earth to procreate. If it didn't feel so damn good, there wouldn't be an overpopulation problem.

He liked sex. Liked it a lot. And it was true what they said about music and girls. Rick did better than he did—Rick liked to say there was something about a man with a guitar that made girls hot. And Percy pranced around like he was a rock god, when he was more like a rock wannabe god. Too loud when he should be soft, too soft when he should be loud. If he made love the way he sang, it was no wonder he had a different girl every week. After one night with him, the girls didn't want another one.

The girls called Sam back. Even though he warned them he was leaving soon, they wanted more of him.

Callie's face blanked. "Take me home."

Coldness grabbed onto his bones. Ice encased his heart.

Laughter seeped through the closed van windows. It was in the low fifties outside. Cold, but nowhere near as cold as his heart. From the rearview mirror, he could see a couple holding hands as they strolled down a row of cars, gazing at each other as if they were newlyweds. But he recognized them as his aunt and uncle, his dad's older brother, who'd been married nearly twenty-five years.

Something tightened inside him.

"Wait," he said and heard his voice crack, and he felt her frown. He knew if he looked at her he would see her brow furrowed with puzzlement. Only when his uncle's car engine started up did he put his hand to the key in the starter...and then he drew the key out. He turned to her, his hands clenching the key, the uneven ridges digging into his palm.

"You realize no matter what happens, I'm leaving tomorrow? I can't stay here. I don't belong here anymore."

She nodded, her gaze on his face. The lights in the parking lot dimmed, leaving her face shadowed. Unreadable.

But he felt her emotions, as if they were live things reaching out to him. "I'll be struggling. I can't commit."

"I'm going to college in the fall." Her voice was husky. "I'm not ready for commitment, either."

"You're sure?"

"Is it that hard to say yes?" She laughed and it came out flat. "I didn't know you were so..." She didn't finish, flapping a hand. "Reluctant. That's not what I've heard."

"I've heard about you, too" he said. What he didn't say that he'd been keeping tabs on her. Not a stalker thing—just out of curiosity. "I'm not a virgin, but I thought you were."

He felt a charge of energy from her, but he couldn't read it.

"Would that make a difference?" she asked.

"I think so."

She gave a harsh laugh. "In that case, you'll be happy to know that I'm not a virgin."

5

Callie held back wild laughter. Amazing that one little word could make such a difference.

Sam ushered her into his bedroom, and she could hear the band playing in the bar below, the music sexy and moody, the thrum vibrating through the floor. The kind of music that lit up a message in her mind, as clear as if it were a neon sign: DO IT NOW. DON'T HESITATE. DON'T SCREW IT UP. THIS MIGHT BE YOUR LAST CHANCE.

She was taking that chance.

So much of her life had been about passing up chances. How could it be any other way? She was the girl with the sick mom.

But this... This she could do. This she *would* do.

He closed the door behind him. She didn't turn to look at him; instead she took in the room: shelves that held a banjo, a half dozen harmonicas, a small drum, a flute, a saxophone, something that could've been a mandolin. A guitar leaned against a corner, a bass guitar in a different corner.

His hand curved around her shoulder. Warm. Branding her with its heat.

Or so it felt, her skin prickling beneath his hand and the prickles spreading down and up her, every inch and every centimeter, like a current of electricity. If he turned off the lights, she wouldn't be surprised if she'd sparkle like an angel on top of a Christmas tree.

His bed was full-sized, and she stared at the musical notes on the black-and-white bedspread. "Nice cover."

His laughter was soft, like a caress. "I think my mother bought it when I was ten."

She twisted to gaze up at him. "It's sweet."

"My mom would hate to be called sweet."

She nodded, though she didn't know his mother well. When they saw each other in the grocery store or the library, they smiled and said hi. His mom wore tight jeans and T-shirts with names of rock bands. In winter, she wore a black leather jacket.

But Callie remembered seeing her in the hall at the elementary school a few days after Sam had broken up with her. She must have looked lost and heartbroken, because Mrs. Krushing had knelt and hugged her and told her she would be all right. She'd said, "When one song stops, another one starts."

"Do you play all these instruments?" Callie asked, still standing, though the bed was about a half foot away from where she stood. She wasn't scared, she just wasn't sure of the protocol. There'd been no making out between them yet. Not even a kiss. Just talking and looking and, most of all, feeling.

"Uh huh. But drums are my favorite."

"Why?" When he didn't reply right away, she tried to read his thoughts in his face. It felt to her that she'd asked him something important. After all, drums mattered to him. Probably more than she did. Maybe more than any girl could.

Oddly, the thought didn't hurt her. For sure, it wasn't going to change her mind.

His forehead worked, as if she'd asked him the meaning of life. Finally, he shrugged. "I guess I like to bang things."

She laughed, and he winced. "I meant the drums. Not you."

"You won't like banging me?" She laughed again, and his eyes sharpened and heated. Her laughter caught in her throat. She hadn't known eyes could look so hot.

She reached up to put her hand on his face— because someone needed to start touching, and he was too slow. She felt the solid bones beneath her fingers, the warmth of his skin as he breathed down at her. She'd never liked it when boys breathed on her face. Which was odd, because Magic had breathed his dog breath at her face so often. She'd always just wrinkled her nose then kissed him. And often she didn't even wrinkle her nose. He was a dog, after all, and it wasn't like he could help having stinky breath.

She'd loved him so much.

She still did. Bodies died, but not love.

"Hey." His voice was so tender it was like being

washed with warm rain water. "Don't cry. We can stop right now."

She blinked hard and sniffed. "I was thinking about Magic."

He pulled her against him. With her heels on, he was about three inches taller than her.

"We can just stay like this," he murmured. "We don't have to do anything."

She closed her eyes and laid her cheek against his shoulder and breathed in his scent. He smelled different from when they were young. He didn't smell like a boy anymore. He smelled like a man.

Only something was wrong. The way he held her wasn't the way a man held a woman he desired. It was...brotherly, and she wanted it to be lover-like.

Except for the long ridge pushing against her belly. That's what gave her the nerve to pull away just enough to look up at him. "But I *want* to do something. I want to do *everything*."

He stared at her, and his lips parted to say something.

"If you ask me if I'm sure again," she said, "I might have to push you on the bed and show you just how sure I am."

He grinned. "You almost tempt me to tell you to show me." His upturned lips flattened, and the tension returned to his face. So did the burn in his eyes, as if he were on fire from the inside out. "But not tonight. Next time, maybe."

Then he bent and kissed her, taking control, his

grip strong yet not hurting. She melted against him. Her whole body seemed to sigh. As if she were coming home. Still kissing her, he drew her down to the bed so he was sitting on it and she was sitting on his lap.

And the kiss went on.

And on.

And on.

In the bar below, a woman belted out a song about how a woman needed a man. Callie didn't always agree with the words. Most of the time she would vigorously denounce them, and a small number of her brain cells that were still operating thought a man must have written the words.

But her body was sending her a different message. She moaned again and held him tightly, and she admitted that right now, she needed a man. And not any man, just *this* man.

He tugged her down, still kissing her, changing their positions so that she lay beneath him on the bedspread with the musical notes. The switch done so smoothly she knew he must have done something similar before. Done it a lot of times.

But right now, she didn't care. Right now, all she cared about was *this*. Him against her. Her arms around him. Her body on fire.

Another song started, a faster one with the drum pounding, and he pulled away slightly, just enough to slide his hand over her dress.

A small sound came out of her mouth, a long

aaah. She knew she should be touching him back, but all she could do was cling to him and moan. His lips left her mouth and feathered down to her throat, finding the sensitive spots, sucking lightly. She moaned and slung her leg around the back of his thigh, holding him close to her, the thickened ridge beneath his jeans pressing between her legs.

The song changed to another, and he shifted down, kissing her below her neck. Her skin felt tender. Her breasts felt tender. Everything about her felt tender, and she squirmed against him.

She needed to get closer to him. Needed to get rid of her clothes.

Yet he took his time, kissing and touching and nibbling while she clutched him and made noises that probably sounded like she had a stomachache.

Another song started, this one slow and seductive, the singer's voice echoing her moans. He lifted his head. "I can't wait much longer."

"Now," she said, her voice hoarse, and the heat inside her grew hotter and higher. Burning. She was on fire. "Right now."

Not waiting for another invite, he rolled off her to take off his clothes.

She didn't wait for him either, sliding off the bed to stand up, already reaching behind her to pull the zipper down. Usually she was so neat. She'd learned to clean up when she was young, so her mom wouldn't have to do it.

But now she let the dress slither down to the wooden floor, and she not only left it there, she dropped her bra and her panties on top of it.

She wished that, for once, she'd worn a thong. Why hadn't she?

The answer came swiftly. Because she hadn't expected to be here with Sam. And because of Magic. She was in mourning for him. She hadn't thought *this* would happen.

Through the miasma of *want*, an ache twisted. Then she caught his gaze on her, and the dull ache vanished. If Magic were here, he would be glad for her. His one wish—after filling his stomach and going for his walk—was for her to be happy.

And now she wasn't precisely happy, she was...burning.

And he...his eyes burned back at her as he lay on the bedspread as if he were a prince and she was the dancer with the seven veils who was here to entertain him.

Her gaze traveled down him from the top of his head to his toes, taking in the beauty of his bare body. His broad shoulders and his lightly muscled chest to his lean hips. And what was between his hips....

She shivered, hot and cold, but mostly hot.

"I hope you like what you see." His voice, heavy with seduction, reminded her of a creamy dessert she'd had once and had been searching for ever since. He patted the bedspread next to her. "The bed's getting cold."

Euphoria and happiness filled her, and she kept her gaze on him. Even with a condom on, his body was a work of art.

"Well?" He grinned and pushed up on his elbows. "Do you want me to come and get you?" His condom-covered penis did a funny little push up, and she laughed then bounced onto the bed. He laughed, too.... And as they stared at each other, the laughter died, and the sexual tension flamed high.

The next second, they were holding each other tightly. Skin slid against skin, and it felt to her like satin rubbing against velvet.

Nothing had ever felt as good. As wonderful. Every nerve ending on her body awake and quivering.

They kissed again, and kissed and kissed as his hands roamed over her body and his erection pushed against her. Then he moved slightly, sliding his hand between her legs, and she could feel his fingers and feel the moisture of her body. And she strained against him, sounds came out of her mouth. "Ooh, oh, oh, oh, oh, oh..."

She still didn't do more than hold on to him, though she knew she should. But this feeling... The pleasure was too intense to respond in kind. Her fingers pressed into skin and muscle, and it was all she could do to keep holding on to him. To keep holding back a scream of pleasure that might be loud enough to penetrate through the floor, and the whole bar crowd below would hear her over the singer's belting voice.

His hand pulled away from her, and she missed it immediately and bit back a cry of disappointment. His touch was so good, and she'd been almost *there*. As if she were the firework, and instead of a wondrous explosion of lights and noise and rapture, she was a dud with just a few sparks.

Then he was between her spread legs, pushing into her, and her thoughts stopped. As he pressed in slowly, she stared at him, and he stared back at her. As if it were important to watch each other. Important for her to see his face flush, his eyes flame, and his pupils darken.

Then she closed her eyes. Better if he didn't see she wasn't reacting the same way.

So this was what it felt like, she thought. Uncomfortable but not hurting.

Something inside her pinched, and she gasped, and then he pushed in all the way, and he made a funny sound. A moan meeting a growl.

Her eyes opened. For a split second, the flame in his eyes blinked out, and a small frown creased his forehead.

Her arms came up to hold him. "It's good," she said. "It's good, it's good." She smiled up at him, feeling him inside her, filling her, pressing against her. It felt...right.

She flexed her muscles.

45

His frown disappeared.

She laughed. Triumphant. "It's *very* good."

He groaned again, and his mouth twisted as if he was in pain. Holding his upper body up, he moved and moved, and she bent her legs and braced her body to take his thrusts.

That delicious feeling she had before didn't come back, but it was still good, and she realized her body was created to do this.

With Sam, she thought. Her body was made to do it with him.

The song changed and another started. She had small moments of wonder, enough to make her cry out softly, but no glorious explosions. As the song ended and another song began, this one faster and louder, he shuddered inside her. His neck corded, and he lifted his head up as he pulsed inside her, his face twisting as if he were hurting, so she thought maybe ecstasy must be a lot like pain.

Slowly, he lowered himself onto her, the pulsing stopped. His chest was heated and sweaty, and the sweat transferred to her skin. But he'd been doing all the work. For her part, she'd mostly squirmed and moaned, her hands flattened against the headboard to keep his powerful thrusts from banging her head into it.

She held him until his rapid heartbeat slowed, even as she wondered whether a heartbeat that fast was good for him. But she'd heard on a talk show that sex several times a week was great exercise for men and women, so she supposed it must be.

He rolled off her and stretched out next to her, relaxed and almost torpid. Like a jungle animal that had been dangerous but was tamed now. At least, for a short while.

The music stopped below. She turned her head. "Will your parents come up?"

He shook his head as another song started. This one a male singer, the music smoother and perfect, clearly not a live performance. "The band's on break, that's all."

"Good."

He looked over at her. "You lied to me about your experience."

"If I'd said I hadn't done this before, you wouldn't have made love to me." She gestured to encompass them and the bed and the bedroom, and everything that had happened in it. "Right?"

"Yes."

"Would you rather I'd done it the first time with someone else?" She watched him, feeling detached, as if his answer didn't matter. "I wish I'd known," she said, before he could reply. "I might have asked Ken to take care of that matter last weekend. I'm sure he wouldn't have had any qualms."

His eyes flamed, and he stared at her. She tensed but didn't look away.

"It's not my business." The heat that had flared in his eyes cooled, but she saw something else.

Something she couldn't name. Or didn't want to. "But I'm glad it wasn't Ken."

Love.

That's what she'd seen in his eyes.

Her breath sucked in.

It couldn't be right. Shouldn't be.

Yet all these years later, she hadn't loved any other boy but him.

Was it possible he felt the same?

"I'm not regretting what we did," he continued while her throat closed up, and she was unable to say anything, afraid if she did, it would come out as a squeak. "The only thing I regret is that you didn't enjoy it more."

"I enjoyed it." Her voice did squeak then, and his lips curved into a smile that sobered quickly.

"Not as much as you will with someone else. After I'm gone."

"Tomorrow," she whispered. He was leaving tomorrow.

He nodded. "We have bad timing."

She slid out of the bed.

"Are you okay?" he asked.

"A little sore." She grabbed her panties. "I had my wisdom teeth pulled out last month. That was much worse."

There was no reply as she stepped into her panties and pulled them up. She looked at his pained expression and burst into laughter. He smiled with a grimace and shook his head while she chuckled.

But inside...inside, the hurt already started.

He got out of bed to get dressed, too. They each used the bathroom then went downstairs and got into his van, and he drove her home, neither saying anything, the radio not even playing.

"You can say something," he said as they neared the city limits. "Ask me anything."

Are you coming back? The question hovered in her mind. "Where are you going?" she asked instead. "L.A.? Memphis? Chicago? New Orleans?"

"You know your blues places." He shot her a quick look that made her feel inordinately smart, though the only reason she paid attention to the cities that were meccas for blues music was because of him. "Rick and I decided to go to Memphis. If the competition is too fierce, we'll try some of the clubs along the delta. Nashville is an option, too. We have more of a country blues vibe than straight blues."

"You'll be a big success." They'd almost reached the edge of the city. Her house wasn't far away, and her belly clenched. This was going too fast.

"I hope you're right." He turned into the lane where she lived, still remembering it all these years later. "And you'll be going to UW-Madison to be a librarian. You always loved books. You'll be a great librarian."

She hadn't told him that, so he must have been keeping up on her, just as she'd kept up on him.

The thought cheered her.

They reached her home. The lights in the living room were on, her mom waiting up for her, and maybe her dad, though she was eighteen. A woman now, not a girl anymore. And often the pain kept her mom up, so she might not really be waiting for her.

He parked in the driveway and turned to her. She leaned over and kissed him. Immediately she wanted him again, but he was the one who put his hands on her upper arms and pulled back.

"We can't do it here," he said.

She looked at him, and the love still inside her grew and expanded. Seeming to fill all the spaces of her body until she was made of pure love.

She put her hands on each side of his face, and words flowed from her. As if they came from somewhere deep in her mind, like water from a river pouring into the ocean.

"I never stopped loving you. I won't be sorry for what happened. I'll think about it often. My love will go with you." She shook her head and laughed a little. "It won't be a jealous, clinging love. It will be just love that wants you to be happy and joyful and successful in whatever you do." She smiled, even as tears filled her eyes, and they were happy tears mixed with sad. "And whoever you do it with."

His mouth opened, and she leaned forward and kissed him hard on the lips, stopping any words he might say. Then she turned and opened the door.

Clutching her purse, she jumped out, pushed the door shut, then ran toward the back of her house.

In a movie, that would be the end of the scene. The end of the movie. But it was real life, and in real life, tears dripped down her face, and she didn't want him to see them.

She heard his car door open, and she ran faster, reaching the back door, her hand on the handle.

"I never stopped loving you, either," he yelled, his voice hoarse, as if he had tears, too. "And I want you to be happy, too."

The tears ran down faster, and she opened the door and hurried inside, closing the door behind her. The kitchen light leaked into the back hallway where all their hooks to hold their jackets were. She leaned against the back door, hardly daring to breathe as she listened to the car back out of the driveway.

"Callie?" her mom called, and she could hear the pain in her mom's voice and knew it was a bad night. She took a deep breath and took out a tissue then wiped her cheeks and blew her nose and sniffed back any more tears.

Putting a smile on her face, she headed into the kitchen. If her mom asked about the graduation party, she would tell her it was fine.

And it was. She glowed inside.

He loved her.

They couldn't be together, but she would always have that.

6

Five years ago...

The high from opening for one of the top country singers of the year was still revving up Sam's nervous system when he and Rick and Rick's girlfriend walked out of the New Jersey theater's side door. Even the cool air hitting him in the face felt good, and he inhaled deeply.

Their other three band members had left after their last set to eat or pick up girls or hit a club or whatever. He'd stayed behind because the main band's manager had said he wanted to talk to him, and Rick had stayed because he and the backup singer had a thing going on. More than a thing, but Sam was keeping his mouth shut about that.

He had other things to think about. The manager had asked him to join the band. Holy shit! That was something. Their drummer was quitting to help build a hospital in Haiti, and the band liked him. Liked him a lot.

He knew he was walking on the sidewalk now, because he could hear a stone roll from beneath his leather boot, but it felt as if he were walking several feet above it.

Of course, he'd said no. But, shit. He'd been *asked*. The manager hadn't tried to talk to him into it. Instead, he'd given him his card and said, "In case you change your mind."

Rick had heard, darting him a glance, then away. Not saying anything. Returning his attention to Justen. Right now, they walked in front of Sam, Rick's arm slung around Justen. Her boots with at least four-inch heels put her at the same height as Rick. They made a good-looking pair, though she was prettier, with flawless, olive-colored skin and black hair that curved below her shoulder blades. She sang like a Siren that lured sailors to their death, and she looked like one, too, with long legs instead of a mermaid's tail.

In Sam's mind, though, he saw a woman a few inches shorter, with an ivory complexion and blue eyes instead of brown doe eyes. She didn't sing well, but her laughter was the best music he'd ever heard.

Regret twisted in his chest.

Almost five years since he'd last seen her, and he missed her. Missed her like hell.

He must've relived the hour with her in his bedroom about five thousand times. She was going to be a librarian, his mom said. She'd been working at the South

Eagleton Library since she was sixteen. The purchasing librarian was going to retire soon, and she'd already been told she would have the job if her grades kept up.

Of course her grades were going to keep up, he'd thought but hadn't said. He'd missed her on his trips home. He traveled most of the summers—in fact, most of the year. And she was in college except for the summer. She was probably sleeping right now. She—

An ear-splitting squeal sliced through his thoughts. They'd reached the front sidewalk, and a group of girls and young women rushed toward them. Someone said, "It's not *them*." Her voice held all the bitterness of a bad-tasting medicine.

There must've been over a dozen, and it was clear by their hunched shoulders they'd been standing in the cold for a while, waiting for the big names. It was March, and in the forties, so none of them were in danger of freezing. Most of them halted, but one kept coming toward them, her hips swaying and her eyes big, a blond who wore her leather coat unbuttoned. The better to show her low-cut top with her boobs half hanging out.

"I know you." The words came out slurred, and she pointed at Rick. "You're the singer."

"That's me," Rick said. They'd had so much trouble keeping singers who tried to run the band but didn't know shit about music that Rick had ended up being their lead singer. He could sing in tune, and it was working out pretty damn well for them. Not enough to get them to the top tier yet, but they thought they were close, so close that the stragglers from last year's A- and B-lists could feel their hot breaths. A few hundred thousand other bands probably thought the same thing.

The blond kept walking toward them, and a brown-haired woman with a roundish face grabbed her arm, her clear whisper carrying. "Farah, he's with someone."

"I don't give a shit." She jerked her arm out of the plainer friend's hold. She put her hand to her hair, and her strut exaggerated, screaming, *Here I am, and ain't I hot? Ain't I ready? Ain't I the woman who will do anything you want?*

Rick shook his head. "Sorry, lady. I'm taken."

"Yes, he's taken," Justen said in a voice like velvet wrapped around steel.

The blond stopped and teetered. Sam suspected it wasn't Rick's comment that did it but Justen's don't-mess-with-my-man voice. That wasn't a tone of voice any sane person would ignore. Apparently it even worked when the person she was talking to was wasted.

The woman's attention turned to Sam. "You're not taken." She headed toward him, her eyes glittering.

A shudder ran up his spine. He held up his hands, shaking his head. "I am."

"Whoever it is, she's not here now." The blond's eyes glittered brighter and harder. She was only a few feet away and still coming toward him. "And I am."

"Farah," the other girl said, a moan in her voice and red blotches on her face.

"You're not going to pass up *this*." The blond pulled up her top, her breasts hanging out.

Jesus. He stepped back, and he heard Justen snort again. He held out his hands then dropped them. This skank might actually run her breasts into his palms.

"Don't they look good?" she asked, jutting them out, her nipples pebbling in the cold air.

He stepped back, and the woman lunged for him. Grabbing his jacket sleeve, she breathed brandy fumes at his face. "Wait! You can have both of us." She swept her hand toward her friend. "Show him! She's not as pretty as me, but her boobies are awesome."

It was like a bad nightmare. The lighting dimmed one half of the friend's face, but the half he could see looked sickly.

"Don't," he said...but she was already pulling up her top, her hands trembling, exposing her breasts. Round and perfect-looking, but, *oh Christ*, the smile she tried to make was a grimace of humiliation, and her hands on her top shook.

He jerked out of the blond's grip, stepped over to the

brunette, and tugged her top down. "You do have a beautiful body, but you don't need to show it to me, and I think you are pretty." He buttoned her coat as she sobbed so quietly no one but him must have heard. She glanced down at the sidewalk that was speckled with age and dirt, and he spoke softly to the top of her head. "It's not you. I've got something else on my mind."

"Me, right?" the blond said. "You've got me on your mind."

He stepped back and turned toward Justen and Rick. "No thanks. Not interested."

There were titters from the other women who were huddled by the brick front of the theater, sheltering from the wind and watching a bonus show.

"Bastard!" the blond shouted.

He, Justen, and Rick started walking away from them. He didn't look back. The next second, something slammed into his back, then glass shattered on the sidewalk.

"Shit." He twisted to glance behind him, and so did Rick and Justen. A bottle was shattered on the concrete, and he could smell brandy that matched the blond's breath.

"Crazy bitch," Justen called. "You do that again, and I'm calling nine-one-one."

"Let's go." The friend was pulling the blond away,

her voice pitched high. "We can't go to jail."

"Bastard, bastard, bastard," the blond yelled, then she turned and ran in the opposite direction with her friend.

"Shit," Sam said again.

Rick laughed. "Man, that's a taste of the big time even I don't want."

Justen jabbed his shoulder. "You better not want it."

"Why would I want the dregs," he said, "when I've got the cream right here?"

Justen laughed huskily, and they headed down the block. Usually the band slept in their vans or with friends, but tonight they were sleeping at a hotel a few blocks down. He and Rick were sharing a room, but he had the feeling he could end up staying with Lenny, who'd played lead guitar since Rick had become the band's singer, and Frank, their keyboardist.

Another yell came to him from the blond, farther away, but he was already mentally dismissing the two women, thinking about Callie being a librarian.

He sang softly, "She loves books, I love her. I see her in the library's aisles, and she always greets me with a smile. In the pages of my mind, she's filed in...in...."

"Ultra fine."

His head snapped up. Rick was grinning at him.

"Super fine," Justen said. "Or mighty fine."

"Mighty fine," Rick said. "I like it. Hey, good one,

Sam. Good tune, too. That's gotta go on the next album. Who doesn't love a librarian?"

"I never met one I didn't like," Justen said.

Sam shrugged. Being stuck in a library would be his worst nightmare.

Unless Callie was with him. Then it would be his best dream.

Rick grinned, as if he read his mind. He slapped Sam on the back of his shoulder. "From bare boobs to librarians. It's a hell of a ride."

"And it's only just beginning," Justen said.

They continued walking, and Sam thrust his hands in his pockets. He wondered if the song would make the cut. If it did, and if Callie heard it, what she would think?

7

Eleven months ago...

Paul pulled his Volkswagen up to the curb, and Callie put on her knit hat and gloves then hurried out of her house before he could get out of the car. They were going to be late for dinner with her parents. Of course she didn't blame him. He'd been showing a home on Angel Lake to a couple. He was an ambitious man. She knew that from their first meeting at a friend's birthday party, when he tried to convince her to let him sell her 1400-square-foot, two-story 1950s house, telling her he knew the perfect condo for her. He liked to joke that he didn't get the listing, but he'd gotten the girl.

She'd laughed the first few times she'd heard it. The joke was getting stale, but she knew she had her annoying habits, too. Who didn't?

Half listening to Paul complain about the hard-to-please couple and half to the slow love song on the radio, she noticed her neighbor's Christmas decorations. Decorations were already on sale at all the stores. Paul had advised her to wait until after the holidays when she'd get them for up to eighty percent off, but she planned to go shopping on Sunday. It was her money, and she didn't want to wait.

A note of excitement in the DJ's voice brought her attention to the radio. "...By two local boys," he said. "Rick Frantzen and Sam Krushing."

She started to reach out to raise the volume but pulled her hand back. Paul was still talking, and she had the feeling she shouldn't reveal her interest.

Not that there was anything to reveal. That one night with Sam had been almost eight years ago. They'd practically been kids. He probably never thought about her.

"The title is 'The Librarian,'" the DJ said.

Her breath sucked in. *Oh my God, oh my God, oh my God.*

"We're here." Paul's voice broke into her thoughts, and he steered into the driveway. "Only twenty minutes late. Not too bad."

Shut up, she thought. *Why don't you shut your big pie hole up?*

But she gave him a tight smile. She could barely hear the lyrics anyway, her nerves jumping all over the place, her head buzzing.

The first thing she'd do when she got home tonight was go to her computer and Google the song.

A second before he took out the key, she heard, *"naked in the stacks."* As she got out of the car, her heart was pounding and her hands shaking. And as much as she tried to pull herself together, it didn't work.

* * *

The band's bus swayed, but Sam kept his eyes closed, and there wasn't any smash, so Bruno, their manager, must've gotten back in the lane. All the while, he never missed a beat, singing Sam and Rick's librarian song off key and with vigor in his drunken-frog voice.

The ones who couldn't do didn't always teach. Some of them became managers who tortured the band with their singing.

The bus swerved again.

And their driving, he added and opened his eyes. He was in the back seat of the bus as they drove to their gig in Decatur. They were supposed to start in three hours, and the sky was already growing dark. He'd been up early and could usually sneak in a nap. Not today, with his mind whirling.

Their album was out, and the critics had listened to it and were commenting.

That was something in itself. Their last album had only caught the attention of their family members and their fans—especially his crazy stalker. The one who claimed on their website's message board that she'd thrown another fan down a flight of steps at a concert in Denver because the fan had thrown her arms around him as they were leaving and had kissed him.

It was true that a fan had fallen down the steps, but she'd been drunk and apparently hadn't been hurt badly. There was no proof that anyone had pushed her, and it was possible his stalker was making it up.

But it hadn't been the first incident, though they'd kept the first incident quiet. That had been a few years back, when it had sure the hell felt like no one cared about them....

Except perhaps his stalker.

And then there'd been the other one. The one he didn't like to think about...the bad one....

He changed his thoughts. Rick said this new album was going to get them all stalker fans. Sam always tightened his lips at the stalker mention, but he hoped Rick was right about their recognition. The DJs loved the album, and so did their fans. The song they really loved was Sam's librarian song.

It had taken him three years to let the band record it. He didn't know why, as if the song was meant for him only. Or maybe he'd been waiting for the right time. The video of Rick following Justen through the stacks of a library was going viral. Every time he looked at YouTube, the views jumped another ten thousand.

It was a hit! A fucking hit! Okay, not a hit yet, but it had been released only a few days ago, and people were noticing and texting and putting it up on social media.

There had to be a hell of lot of guys with librarian fantasies.

Bruno finished the song and this time didn't start again, making Sam think life was already getting better. He shifted in his seat, looking forward. Justen and Rick sat in the middle of the bus, murmuring to each other. At one point, Sam would've put money down on a bet that he'd be the one who'd find a woman first, and Rick would be last. But when Rick had met Justen, he was a goner. That was it for him. She left her backup singing gig to become part of the band—singing with Rick sometimes, and other times singing backup to him, and other times he'd be her backup. They all benefited.

Lenny and Frank sat a few rows ahead of Rick and Justen. Lenny had on headphones, and Frank was emailing his wife, who'd just found out she had ovarian cancer.

Life could be a bitch.

Tension from all his thoughts, all the possibilities, good and bad, made Sam's fingers twitch. He wanted to do what he did best. Not putting on headphones. He was too hyped to sit still and listen to music. He needed his drums. Needed to bang on them until the tension rolled right out of him.

His cell phone trilled the three notes he'd set up for his mom. He put it to his ear and said hi.

For the first time that he could remember, she

squealed. "They played your song on the radio!"

"It's not the first." Songs from their last studio album had been on the radio quite a few times, but they were like rain drops getting lost in the mist.

"It's the first one they've made a big deal out of. The DJ said it's going to be big."

"I hope your DJ is right."

"Honey, you deserve this."

"Me and tens of thousands of other bands."

"You're good."

He nodded. But they had to be better than good. They had to know people. Or be outrageous. Or be lucky. Or just be so amazingly good that people couldn't ignore them.

He didn't know just what they were, but he liked to think their band had a little of all of that: Shock, awe, talent, and perseverance.

"I wonder what a certain librarian will think about your song," his mom said.

"I don't know what you're talking about."

"Sure, honey. You keep telling yourself that."

He grimaced. They talked for a few minutes more then hung up. The tiredness caught up with him, and so did the melancholy.

It had been eight years since that night with Callie. He hadn't seen her since. He'd changed since then. She must've changed, too. If he saw her and talked to her, she'd probably bore him. They probably had nothing in common. She probably wouldn't remember that night in his bedroom above the bar, making love and saying to him, "My love will go with you."

He'd never forgotten that night.

He'd never forgotten her words.

They haunted him.

He closed his eyes again. He didn't know if anyone else but his parents would love him that much. Not him as a drummer, country rocker, and songwriter. But him, the man, with all his faults. Not even caring about his talents. As if she'd love him if he were a cook in a diner.

But that was eight years ago. More than a third of his life. Sure, he'd been touring, and she had gone to the university in Madison. But he'd had gigs in Madison and had never seen her there. Other kids he'd known from Eagleton had called or tweeted him, and he'd sent them free tickets. But not her.

It was apparent she'd gone on with her life.

He needed to go on with his, too.

That was the real reason he'd let go of the song.

Maybe now he could let another woman into not just his bed but his life, too.

"Hey, Sam," Justen called. "You got another one."

He opened his eyes but remained slouched in his seat. "Another what?"

"Another tweet from your Number One favorite fan and wannabe wife."

He groaned.

"She's pissed at all the other women who are after you now." Rick laughed. "She said you're hers and have been for years now. She's not going to let anyone else have you."

"She's a wack job."

"Scary is what she is," Justen said. "Rick, read him the rest."

"Sam, I know you're reading this," Rick said in a falsetto. *"Next time you won't turn me down. I'm making sure of it."*

"Crazy blond." He scowled. The person calling herself MrsSamKrushing—no punctuation or spaces, according to his friends—had been doing this for four years. Who kept an obsession that long?

"You sure it's the blond from Jersey?" Justen asked.

"She's the one I turned down."

"The one that threw the bottle at his back." Rick nodded at Lenny. "You should've been there with us. You could've had her."

"If she'd had a gun..." Turned in his seat, his headphones around his neck now, Lenny pointed his index finger at Sam, his thumb in the air. With a narrowing of his eyes, he gestured like he was pulling a trigger. "Bang, bang, you're dead."

"Thanks a lot, Len."

"Always glad to help." Lenny grinned then shrugged. "You can't be sure it's her. You turn down most of the girls who come on to you. It's not like your crazy fan girl sent a picture. But if you're scared, call the cops. I would. She's starting to get creepy."

"If she hasn't threatened him," Justen said, "or broken into his hotel room or the bus, or anything like that, the police won't do anything. They didn't do anything when the two girls were shoved down the steps."

"They couldn't prove anything," Rick said. "And they didn't want to bother. No one saw anything, and the one girl had been drinking."

Lenny exhaled a heavy breath. "I've known a few crazy blonds, and when they get angry..." Making a sound like an exploding bomb, he gestured like his head was blowing up.

"There are a lot of crazy blonds in the world," Rick said.

"And brunettes, redheads, and"—Lenny winked at Justen—"black hair."

"More of the crazy ones come with a penis than a uterus." Justen scowled, giving Rick a scathing look that didn't bode well for their imminent sexual activity. "Testosterone is the war-making hormone."

"Babe, it's more well-known for baby making." Rick's eyebrows cocked. "You wanna try?"

"Seriously?"

He stared at her. The atmosphere changed, the air heating. In his bus seat, Sam sat up straight. The radio up front went silent, Bruno listening as he drove. Lenny was staring. The only one not paying attention was Frank, bent over, talking on his cell phone, too low for them to hear. His posture was tense, his attention far away from Sam, Justen, Rick, and the others.

In that second, when everyone else's attention was on Rick and Justen, Sam *knew*. Frank was going to quit the band—just as they were on the verge of making it big.

Or falling on their faces again.

Damn. Sam was going to miss Frank. He was quiet and dependable and good. And he didn't bring any drama to the group, even with all his indecision. Wanting to be with his wife and two kids, and wanting to make music. Torn between two loves, and it looked like family was winning.

For a long moment, Sam envied him.

Especially since the stalker's tweets really did seem more frantic lately. Darker and grimmer. As if she'd lost hope. And he didn't know if she was the blond, or what color hair she had. Hell, he didn't know if she was a he. All he knew was that she was trouble, and he wanted her/him/it out of his life.

Rick laughed softy, and Sam's attention snapped back to him. "Yeah," Rick said. "I want to make a baby with you."

Justen's breath hissed in, loud enough for Sam to hear. "When we get our Grammy..." She broke off and choked out a laugh that sounded close to a sob. "Then we'll do it."

Rick grabbed her hands. "Baby, I like the way you think."

"You better." Her voice was low and fierce. "I'm going to be your baby mama."

"What if it doesn't happen with this album?" Rick frowned.

"Backing out already?" she asked.

"No way. I'm in all the way."

"I think we'll have that Grammy with this one, but if not"—she smiled, and Sam felt invisible lights of joy pinging out of her—"...then we'll just have to practice the baby making. So when the time comes, we'll get it right."

Rick threw back his head and laughed, and then they kissed. Sam leaned back on his seat, not comfortably, because the bus was made for transportation not comfort. Though it had been eight years, he thought again of Callie, and he felt the emptiness inside him. A big black hole. As he stared ahead, in his head, he heard Rick sing, *"The librarian, the librarian, I'm a barbarian in love with the librarian."*

He closed his eyes tight, unable to deny that she was still locked inside his heart....

8

The men were in the living room, watching a basketball game on TV. Usually Callie's dad helped clean up, but not tonight. She cleared the table, thinking he probably wanted some alone time with Paul to probe into his character. She didn't bring many men home—Paul was only the second one—and her dad probably thought she was serious.

Was she? She didn't know. She'd thought they were on that road, and then in the car, she'd heard the news about Sam...

Using a dirty knife, she scraped bits of food into the garbage bag under the sink. Just past the city limits, they had their own septic and well, and her parents preferred to compost their food. When she straightened, she saw her mom leaning over the dishwasher, putting dishes in it.

Callie frowned. Something was wrong with this picture. It took a second to realize her mother wasn't loading the dishwasher with one hand, the other holding on to the counter in case she lost her balance.

"Mom!"

Her mother looked up, one eyebrow raised. "Yes?"

Callie's heartbeat quickened. She set the plate

on the counter then wiped her hands on the sides of her jeans. "You seem different. Healthier. Are you smoking weed?"

Her mom lifted both eyebrows.

"You can tell me." She narrowed her eyes. Now that she thought about it, her mom had been moving better lately, and her features weren't pinched from holding back pain. "All I want is for you to be better. If marijuana accomplishes that, I'll buy it for you myself."

"It's not that." Her mom's smile was wide, and she stood straight instead of leaning against the counter. "I didn't want to tell you before, in case it would be a disappointment. Or if it made me worse."

"In case *what* did?" She closed the cupboard door and stepped toward her mom. Her heart beat even faster, as if she'd run a mile. She knew enough about marijuana to be pretty sure it wouldn't make her mother's health worse. What was going on?

"I'm on another clinical trial." Her mother's smile was serene. "And this one seems to be working."

"Mom!" She lunged for her mom and wrapped her arms around her, holding her gently when she wanted to grip her tightly.

Her mother laughed low in her throat. Callie closed her eyes and heard the announcer on TV saying something, then Paul and her dad saying something back.

For that second, everything seemed to be just right. Perfect.

Except for the yearning inside her...

If only Sam's band hadn't written a song about a librarian.

She hugged her mom harder then stepped back. "What do you think about Paul?"

"Well..." Her mom shook her head. "He's fine. Just fine."

"You don't like him?" She raised her eyebrows. She'd thought Paul would be the exact kind of man her parents would love. He had a secure job in the real estate agency. He had plans for the future. He didn't go clubbing. He had opinions on schools and how people should behave. He was a devoted Packers fan. He even went to church, something Callie didn't do every week, not when she had a good book to read. And since she worked in a library, she had a lot of good books to read. She often thought they gave her lessons in right and wrong. And romances gave a lesson that love was better than hate. In fact, love could be the best thing ever.

Her mom frowned. "We just met him today, and he seems fine. You know your dad and I want the best for you."

"I deserve the best." She grinned.

"You do." Her mom's expression remained somber. "Are you and he serious?"

"We've been dating for three months, and we haven't had any arguments. We agree on almost everything. We haven't fought once."

"Three months isn't long. And he doesn't seem like the kind of man to jump into anything."

Callie shook her head. She wasn't the kind of woman to jump into anything, either. Not anymore. She'd jumped twice. The first time, she was four, and a boy had asked her to marry him.

That had led to the second time she'd jumped.

Closing her eyes, she thought of the night of the graduation party, with her and Sam in the bed above his parents' bar. She grew warm. She hadn't just jumped into bed with Sam; she'd jumped into love with him.

"Are you all right?" Her mom frowned at her.

She nodded and opened her eyes. She reminded herself that she hadn't experienced the big O with Sam that night. Nor with any man since him, either. Maybe worse, she'd experienced the big love.

But that was in the past. She needed to get over it. He was a memory. The cells of the human body regenerated every seven years, so she was a different woman from the one she'd been then. He must be different, too.

She'd grown, had met different people, had sex with a few different men. She knew he must have had sex with many more women. He'd traveled the country, and his mother liked to say that he'd been everywhere.

Except for short trips to Madison, Milwaukee, Chicago and Minneapolis, her one big trip had been to visit her aunt and uncle in Arizona. She'd gone with her mom and dad. She didn't lead an exciting life. Maybe that was why she wouldn't let go of the memory. If she met Sam now, they would realize they had nothing in common.

And maybe the librarian song wasn't about her. Maybe he'd written that song for an entirely different woman.

"Honey?" her mom said.

She opened her eyes. "All my friends from high school are married."

"A couple are divorced already," her mother said. "Julie Rhymer has two toddlers and a deadbeat ex."

"I know." Their church had held a giant rummage sale to raise money for her. When Julie had stood in front of the congregation, thanking them and crying, Callie had cuddled her youngest boy, a baby then, and smelled the baby scent. The smell and feel had tugged at her heart.

She'd stupidly wondered what her and Sam's children would have looked like.

When she'd gone home, she'd written a poem about it.

"I have to go on with my life," she said.

"Don't do anything you'll be sorry for."

"Mom, everyone does things they're sorry for."

She smiled but felt it wobble. "I think the worst thing to be sorry for would be to be so afraid of making a mistake you don't do anything."

Her mother put her hands on each side of her face. "Promise me you'll wait a year. Promise."

Callie stared at her a long moment before nodding. When she did, it felt as if a weight lifted from her shoulders. A whole year.

Anything could happen.

9

One month ago...

"And the Grammy goes to..." The redheaded singer with the barely there dress looked out at the audience with some of the biggest names in the music world.

Amazingly, Sam Krushing was one of the audience members. Sitting near the aisle in case he and the others got to jump up for one of the three awards Got Mojo was up for.

Three! Three of them! Three fucking nominations!

It was...the best. After nine years and almost making it so many times that he'd begun to think it might never happen, that they'd always be passed by...they'd clicked with their last blues-country album. It wasn't that they'd finally found listeners. Instead, it was listeners who'd found them.

But was it enough?

So far, winners of two of the categories they were up for had already been announced, and neither name had been theirs.

This was their last chance. A fat chance, too. Or would that be slim? Up against four big hitters. In baseball, the others would be in the Major Leagues and they'd be in the Minors. Their chances of winning were as small as the hearts of most music company executives.

He felt as if he were floating above the seats. What was taking the singer so long? Was she waiting to make sure everyone got a peek at her assets? It wasn't anything any of them hadn't seen before. And he was pretty sure they weren't real, either. Real ones just had a different look to them than fake. A different feel.

He should write a song about breasts. Rick and him. After all, Rick had more experience than him. Not since Justen, though. Rick had been a lucky man to find her. They—

The singer's red-lipsticked lips opened, and his mind froze, his muscles bunching.

"Got Mojo," she said.

A roar rose up, but it sounded muted, a buzzing in his hears, and he was the guy who heard everything. Rick jumped to his feet, hugging Justen, smacking a big one on her lips.

Sam was on his feet, too, and he couldn't recall getting up from his chair. Hell, they hadn't even been invited to perform, so he'd been sure they'd walk out as empty-handed as when they'd walked in. There were too many of the big names, the cool rappers, former Disney stars turned singers, guys who danced, and girls who had millions of teen fans who wanted to look and sing just like them.

Lenny pounded his back, bringing him down to earth. "We did it," he yelled in his ear. "We fucking did it."

Lenny pulled him into the aisle, and as they walked up, people called out their congrats and reached out to touch them, as if some of the winning magic would rub off on them.

Then they were on the stage, and he wasn't sure how they'd gotten there, though logic told him they'd walked up. The singer who'd announced them, the one who'd made him think about fake boobs, kissed him. Not a small smack but a want-you-as-my-lover smack. The audience whooped and clapped, then she let him go, her eyes gleaming, either because she was on something or because of the attention.

Not caring which, he turned in time to see Rick kiss his Grammy and thank all the fans and then their label. While Rick spoke, Sam looked at the audience, and there were a lot of people he idolized and some his parents had idolized. And, oh man, he was here in front of them. It didn't seem real.

Then Lenny shoved him in front of the mike. Sam held up his Grammy and yelled, "This is for the all the librarians!"

The audience roared, even as he took in the irony that he could barely read and had only been in the library a few dozen times with his mom when she picked up an audio book for him.

But at least he hadn't said, "one particular librarian."

Not that anyone would pay attention...except his mom.

But he wondered if Callie was watching. He wondered if she knew.

Their time was up, the cameras switching to a boy band on another stage, and they walked off to have their pictures taken. It all seemed surreal, though he tried to be in the moment. This was what they all had hoped for. There was no going back now. From this point on, he was only going forward....

* * *

The singer wearing the almost-not-there dress, pressed her body against Sam like she was a hot steam iron and he was a wrinkled pair of jeans.

Callie curled her fingers into tight fists. On the couch next to her in her living room, Paul chortled. She stared ahead, not saying anything, certainly not giving in to her impulse to accidentally spill his wine on him. After all, it might stain her couch.

She didn't think about Sam all the time. She had a life. She had work she loved. She had friends and a family. She even had a boyfriend. And she hadn't seen Sam in nine years. Nine long years.

The first five years after she'd turned eighteen, he'd visited his parents in the winter when she was at school in Madison. The band's busiest touring times were in the summer, she knew that. Though, from occasionally looking at their website on late nights when she couldn't sleep, she saw they toured most of the year.

They'd played in Madison a few times when she was in college, but she hadn't gone. He knew where she was. If he wanted to see her, he could contact her. Even send her free tickets.

She'd never heard from him, so obviously he didn't want to see her. Maybe he'd forgotten about her.

Except there was that song... Lyrics by Sam Krushing. Rick shared credits for the music with Sam, but the lyrics for the librarian song were all his.

And she certainly knew Sam wasn't in libraries much, so he couldn't have had much of a love for librarians in general.

She'd thought...hoped...that perhaps he'd sometimes thought of her with fondness. Perhaps even more than fondness.

But when he kissed the woman, she felt sick inside, as if someone had kicked her hard in the belly.

She had no right or no reason to feel that way, but sometimes right or reason didn't matter.

The camera twisted to a band on a different stage, and she turned to Paul. They'd been dating for almost a year now, and she felt...ambivalent about him. He'd shown a few instances of anger, a vein pulsing in his forehead—usually when a sale had fallen through or a client had switched to another agency. But she'd told herself that it showed he was ambitious. Wasn't that what most women wanted in a husband?

Thanksgiving and Christmas had been tense between them when she'd gone to her family's celebrations instead of his. He'd said that *he'd* been willing to compromise...but as he'd spoken, the vein on his forehead had throbbed.

She'd coolly reminded him that they weren't at that point of their relationship, and he'd backed off. She'd forced a smile, her common sense reminding her that she was twenty-seven now.

Wasn't it time for her to stop hoping to magically run into Mr. Perfect?

After all, Eagleton wasn't overflowing with eligible men her age. Most were married already. And the ones that weren't... Usually there was a reason they weren't married.

The other day at the library, she'd been asked out by a man with a comb-over and an extra forty or more pounds that matched his forty or so years. He'd seemed like a nice man, and maybe the woman who eventually got his ring on her finger might be the luckiest woman in Eagleton...but it wouldn't be her.

As she turned to look at Paul now, she noted his attractive appearance with his light brown hair and pleasant features. He would never make her swoon, but neither did he have the "ick" factor. And he worked hard at selling homes and did well. He already owned a four-family house, renting out three units and living in one. He didn't gamble, and he drank and ate in moderation. He didn't have any weird kinks—at least, none that she was aware of.

She couldn't do much better than him.

Or did she mean worse?

She winced, and her heart felt heavy.

He set his empty glass on the coffee table. "This is running late. It's a work day for us tomorrow. I'd better get going."

She felt a vast sense of relief. *Yes, go. Do go.*

Right now, she was glad for him to go. Right now, the image of Sam kissing that trampy singer was burnt in her mind, and it bothered her much more than she had any right to be bothered about it.

She stood, and so did Paul.

"It's been a very nice evening." His voice crooned. "It's always a nice evening with you."

She forced a smile. *Nice* was the right word.

She knew words. She *loved* words. But she didn't love *nice*. What if she wanted *wild*? *Fierce*? *Breathtaking*? *Crazy*? *Sexy*?

"Marry me," he said. "We'd make a good couple."

"Yes," she said, answering the last part of what he'd said. They would make a good couple.

Why was he staring at her with a goofy smile?

And now he was bending down to kiss her.

As their lips touched, she realized she'd said yes to his proposal.

She might have explained her mistake—though saying her mind had been elsewhere probably wasn't something a man wanted to hear after he'd proposed—but his tongue pushed into her mouth.

It would be rude to say no now. To shove him away like he was a boy with cooties.

As they kissed, she felt nothing, though his kiss was pleasant, and at least he wasn't dripping saliva on her. Though one of the library volunteers said slobber on the upper lips was like KY Jelly on the lips below the hips. Made them juicier.

Along with all these thoughts jumping in her mind, she had one more.

What if this was the best she could do?

She wanted children. So did Paul. She'd warned him that any children she might have would be at risk of getting MS, too. His eyes had lit up, as if it were a challenge, and he'd said he wasn't worried. As if his sheer willpower would keep the disease away.

He hadn't even paused. She admired that. She admired that a lot. That was the first time she'd thought she might marry him.

More prosaically, they had similar interests and friends. Similar goals.

So why wait? After all, if she wanted a turbulent, do-anything-for-love romance, she could find it anytime she wanted. All she needed to do was open a book.

When he pulled away, he said, "I have showings

all this week, but next week I'll set aside an evening for us to shop for a ring."

She nodded. Weekends were his busy time. Really, his schedule was fairly busy and they wouldn't see a lot of each other.

Maybe marriage to him wouldn't be so bad.

They walked to the door together, and she was happy that he didn't think an acceptance of his marriage proposal meant they needed to hop into bed tonight. It was late, and they were both tired.

He donned his jacket and, in a low voice with a growl in it, said, "If we didn't have to work tomorrow..."

Before she could think of a reply, he grabbed her and kissed her, holding her closer than usual. With his arms clutching her, she felt suffocated. His kiss was hard, too, bending her head back so her neck hurt.

"We'll celebrate this weekend," he said.

He left, and she stayed in front of the door and wrapped her arms around herself and wondered what she'd just done. Then she remembered she'd promised her mother to wait a year. It wasn't quite eleven months.

Too late, she thought, and she felt a little dead inside. But it wasn't as if anything in her life was going to change. She would marry him. He'd be a good husband. She'd be a good wife. They would have children they'd love fiercely, no matter what challenges they might or might not face.

So what if he had a bit of bombast that she disliked. Nobody was perfect. How could she say no?

It was as much and maybe even more than most people had.

She plunked herself down on the couch. The award show was still on; a man wearing boots and a cowboy hat was singing about fishing and drinking. Though she liked country music, she turned it off then sat there with her eyes closed. Without noise and without Paul's company, her thoughts fluttered away from the proposal.

Instead she pictured Sam on the stage, wearing a black suit and narrow tie, and he'd looked so solid and earthy. She was happy for him, yet her heart twisted inside her chest. Like a little pebble in a favorite shoe that, no matter how hard she shook it out, always seemed to be there.

Which was so ridiculous. He was unattainable. Gone most of the time. Maybe that's why he was easier to keep in her heart. The one that got away. If he'd stayed, she was sure there would be many things about him that would irritate her. He was, after all, a man.

Yet she admitted that after Magic had passed away, she could never bring herself to adopt another dog.

Just picturing the happy smile on Magic's face when he saw her and the pure love in his brown eyes, she felt another twist in her heart.

As stupid as it was, all these years later, she still missed Magic. And she still missed Sam.

She had two holes in her heart that had never healed.

Finally she did the only thing she could. She walked into her office, sat in front of her computer, and opened a new document in the word processing program.

My cracked heart broke again today.
And I did something that might be a mistake.
I wish I had the toughness of Scarlett
The pride and wit of Elizabeth
And most of all, the strong heart of Jo.

Her fingers stilled on the keys. After a moment, she put her head in her hands. Another few moments passed, and she raised her head and turned off the computer.

Why finish the poem? It wasn't as if she was going to do anything with it.

She stood and went to get ready for bed. Tomorrow she would be in a better mood. As for Scarlett, Elizabeth and Jo...well, fiction was so much easier than real life.

10

Present day...

Inside a smallish kitchen in downtown Eagleton, a cat lifted her nose.

Her eyes that had gone dull sparkled. Her fur fluffed out.

The humans who housed her and fed her, day after day, pet food as dry and spare as their hearts, were away from home, leaving her alone once again with just a bowl of stale water.

Everything as usual since she'd been in this place, and she'd been in this place too long. The humans were gone most of the day and parts of the night. They fed her once a day and gave her water. When they were home, they ignored her.

She wasn't important to them.

She didn't matter.

Even though she was young, barely two years in human time, she felt old in spirit. Weighed down.

There had been a mistake. She knew it. She should be someplace else.

But today, something was different. She smelled it in the air.

She couldn't say what was different; all she knew was that a change was coming. Lives would turn upside down. Including hers.

Her senses fully awake, she stared out the window into the darkness. Vigilant.

When it was time for action, she would be ready.

Just as she thought that, cold air whistled into the house.

She padded toward the hall, and as she did, the air grew colder. Along with the wind's whistle came music, and a human male was singing, the sound not unpleasant.

As she neared the door, she saw it wasn't fully closed. The cold wind whistled through the crack straight at her. She leapt back.

She didn't like cold.

A gust shook the door then halted. A calm moment that the cat knew would not last. She could feel the tremble in the air. As she stared at the door, another gust slammed into it, and it did something that shouldn't have happened. The door smashed open.

Before she could react, the door bounced back, banging shut.

In that instant, she knew.

The wind was doing this for her.

Once again, the air trembled. She dashed to the door, not hesitating. She needed to leave. Now. Cold outside or not, this was her chance to escape. Her chance to find the place where she should be.

This time, she would be ready for it. This time, she would act.

If she didn't, there might not be a next time.

The wind gusted at the door again, but it was weaker, only opening a short way and already starting to rebound back.

With a yowl, she shoved her chin and her left front leg into the crack, knowing the door could bang into her and hurt her badly. But she had to try.

As if empowered by her bravery, the wind gusted again. At the same time, she shoved, and with the assistance of the wind, she pushed the door open. Not all the way but just far enough for one slender cat—if she was fast enough.

Not hesitating, she put her head down and dashed out of the silent house devoid of love and joy. Heading straight toward the music. It's what had called her to the door in the first place. Maybe the music would show her the way.

* * *

Sam peered around the bar. His parents and a couple of part-timers were bartending. This wasn't the first time Sam and Rick had come home since they'd left Eagleton for Memphis nine years ago, but it was the first time since the Grammy. Every time Sam thought about the win, he wanted to grab his sticks and do a wild drum roll. The kind that a dervish would dance to then fall down with wild laughter.

It was a Tuesday night or, as his mother called

it, "snooze night." But there was no snoozing tonight. The bar was crammed and hopping, a hell of a lot of people in the city of Eagleton wide awake and gathered to see the unlikely hometown boys who had won the Grammy and mingled with the stars who seemed so far away and glittering. To talk with him and Rick, to take pictures with them, to touch them. As if there were stardust sprinkled on them and, if they got close enough, some of the stardust could shake off onto them, and they would shine brightly, too.

Rick was talking to all the young, hot women, spreading his charm, though Sam was pretty sure that he wasn't dumb enough to go home with any of them. Not when he had Justen, who was visiting her parents in Kentucky.

Sam chatted with the older patrons. He'd grown up with many of the regulars, and they all had stories about Sam as a kid, banging away on the drums—in perfect rhythm—when he was shorter than the cymbals on the stands. A few even brought old photos they held out to Sam to sign, saying they'd known he'd be famous someday.

He was having a good time, even if he didn't believe them. Shortly before ten, his mom let the two part-timers who usually worked the weekends take over while she and his dad and Rick hopped on the stage with their guitars, and he sat in the back with his drums, grinning like a fool. A blond cutie who'd been giving him smoldering looks since she'd sashayed into the bar with hips swinging got on stage to sing one of their songs with Rick, taking on Justen's lines.

Sam's mom leaned into him. "She's good." She winked. "She's pretty, too."

"My mom, the pimp," he said.

She socked him in his bicep with her bony knuckles. He yelped, and she snickered. He thought how young she looked in the dimmer bar light. She was proud to say that her jeans were ten years old, though he suspected she had a harder time snapping them shut. But, bottom line, she still looked good in her jeans, and she and his dad loved music, loved their bar, loved their motorcycles, and loved him.

Rick was saying something to the crowd about dedicating this song to all his homies in the bar, getting effusive and even melancholy—which told Sam he'd been drinking too much. Sam got to his feet, stepped around the drums and, a bit awkwardly, with the guitar between them, he hugged his mom.

"Without you and Dad," he said, loudly enough for everyone to hear, "I'd be barely getting by. I'd be angry and broke and pissed off at the world. I'm a lucky man."

Wild clapping came from the patrons. He stepped back, waved at the crowd that was miniscule compared to the halls they mostly filled now, and stepped back to the drums, picking up his sticks that felt like old friends.

And then he did a fast riff on the snare and a kick on the top hat, and he called out, "Let's make some music!"

Rick stopped talking and started his own powerhouse run on his Fender. After a couple minutes, his mom and dad jumped in. The girl singer stepped back to let them fill the bar with foot-stomping, heart-pounding, rock-tastic music that would shake a zombie out of a stupor.

Once they got that out of their system, like getting that first cup of caffeine-laced coffee into the bloodstream in the morning, they slowed and played a song about lost love. It started with soft waves and ended with a crashing storm. The girl singer belted out the song almost as well as Justen. Once she learned how to control her voice, use it like it was an instrument, she'd be great.

That didn't mean she'd get anywhere. There were a lot of amazing singers in Nashville playing on sidewalk corners for tips.

But for now, he just jammed. Tonight was all about celebration and song. Tonight was about finally making it, and being with the people who loved him even when he was sleeping in the bus on cold, snowy nights and hot, muggy ones, unable to afford to pay for a room. Not if he wanted to eat. Tonight was about spreading the joy.

This could all fall apart by next year, so he damn well wasn't going to pass off the chance to celebrate the good stuff.

As he pounded his drums, the wildness swelled inside him, faster and higher than a Mississippi flood, and he was hip deep in it, banging his drums as if it would keep them from drowning and get them to heaven.

And then he looked up. He didn't know what caught his attention. Not the opening of the door, because the door had been opening and closing off and on all night. Not the smell, because there were too many smells fighting in the place, and that wasn't counting the sweet potato fries the bar specialized in because his mom said they needed some food with the booze, and they may as well make it classy. All he knew was that he looked up straight into the summer-blue eyes of his first girlfriend. The one who'd inspired their first hit song.

He didn't freeze. Instead the joy he'd been feeling intensified, flooding him. And all he could think of was that, after too many years, he was seeing *her* again.

He'd thought she was in the past. A sweet memory that never quite left him. So much had happened since he'd last seen her when he was eighteen. Since the night they'd made love. But his heart slammed against the inside of his chest faster than he was slapping his sticks on the snares, playing another song he'd co-written with Rick on their latest album, titled, "I Want You." It

felt to him that he'd written his part just for her.
For that one June night in the past. For many
nights in the future.

In that instant, he knew that nothing had
changed in the last nine years. That he'd want her
if he had to crawl through an alligator-infested
swamp for her. If he had to brave a hurricane for
her. If she gained one hundred pounds and told
him to his face she never wanted to lose a single
one.

He. Just. Wanted. Her.

Then a hand curved possessively over her
shoulder.

The wave of joy receded, vanished, crashed to
the floor.

She wasn't alone. A slender man about a head
taller than her, with receding, light brown hair,
stood behind her, gripping her shoulder as if she
were a possession that belonged to him.

And the expression in her face wasn't happiness
to see him. It was...anguish.

* * *

Callie crossed her arms, clutching herself, trying
to hold back the emotion flooding her. But that
flood was in full force, and she could no more stop
it than she could stop the moon from shining on
full-moon nights.

She hadn't wanted to come tonight, but Paul

had insisted until she'd given in. She didn't have a good reason to give him to stay away. How could she tell him she was afraid of what would happen?

And she'd been right to be afraid. One look at Sam. That's all it had taken to know she was lying to herself and, worse, lying to Paul.

He was a great guy, and she'd wanted to love him. But she couldn't force her heart to do what it didn't want to do.

She closed her eyes, and the music thrummed through her, transporting her back to the night nine years ago. Not literally, not with her body. But with her mind and emotions, she was in Sam's bedroom above the bar, and he'd been thrusting into her. Though it hadn't lifted her to the erotic heights she read about in romances, it had been sweet and wonderful.

It had been Sam. She hadn't needed more.

The brilliantly clear memory of their lovemaking felt more real than Paul's hand on her shoulder. As if it were happening right now. With her eyes closed, she could feel him, smell him, touch him....

The song stopped, snapping her back to earth. Taking a shuddering breath, she opened her eyes to watch Brenda, Sam's mom, beam at the audience. She looked like a tough biker woman in her jeans and her black Got Mojo T-shirt. Pride for her son's success streamed out of her from every pore. Sam's dad, Roger, was grinning just as widely. Pure happiness for his son.

And Sam... He stared at her. It felt...good. Right. Even though she hurt inside. Because she was just as happy for his success.

Then she looked down at the modest diamond ring circling her left ring finger and told herself the same lie she'd been telling herself for the last few months. That Paul was a man she could love.

A man she could have a child and a family with.

A man who would be there for her when she needed him.

Sometimes she just needed a man to hold her. Sometimes she needed a man in her bed. Sometimes she needed someone to kill wasps for her and change light bulbs in her small house with the ten-foot ceilings so she wouldn't have to climb the ladder to do it herself. And sometimes, when she waited in the hospital or the doctor's office for her mother—the times when her mom was too sick to drive herself and her father was working—she ached to have someone sitting with her in the waiting area, holding her hand.

She'd told herself that she didn't have to love Paul in the soul-bonding way she'd felt for Sam. She'd told herself that she'd been young then. Barely eighteen. And young women imagined their love was forever.

But looking at Sam now, she felt the punch in her stomach. She felt drawn to him, as if an invisible string between them was pulling her toward him.

She forced herself to stand still when every cell in her body screamed at her to shake off Paul's hand from her shoulder and walk toward Sam like a programmed robot.

Instead, she locked her muscles. Not here. She couldn't do it here.

"I'll get us something to drink." He leaned close to talk in her ear so she could hear through the noise.

His breath in her ear made her shudder. It sickened her.

She closed her eyes for one second. As he turned away to get their drinks, she snapped around and grabbed his arm. He glanced back at her.

"I need to talk to you," she said. "Let's go outside."

11

In walked the cat...

"Paul, you're a wonderful man, and I know..." Callie stopped in front of the knitting shop two buildings down from the bar. Far enough that the smokers huddled on the sidewalk in front of the bar wouldn't overhear them. She took a breath of wintry air then continued. "I know that any woman would..." She stopped again, her gaze flickering up to his face then down.

"Jesus! You're breaking up with me!"

Chills prickled on Callie's spine. She didn't like the anger that sharpened his voice. "I have doubts. It's not you, Paul, it's—"

"I don't believe this." He grasped her forearm, and her breath sucked in. "I told my parents and my friends and the other agents that we were getting married. My grandparents are buying a trip to Bali for our honeymoon. My cousin Amy is going to bake the wedding cake—"

"What? We didn't even set a date yet or talk about a cake." She strained away from him, but even with a layer of quilting on her jacket, his grip was digging into her arm. "Let me go, Paul. You're hurting me."

"You can't do this to me." He glared at her.

"We've been dating over a year. You're just getting cold feet. You don't really mean this."

"If I had any doubts, you certainly blew them away with your behavior." She tugged her arm back, but he didn't let go. "Let me go, or I'll scream."

"You don't understand." He spoke in short bursts that hit her ears like fists. "I knew on our first date that you were perfect for me. But you always held back. For this last year, I've felt that I'm walking on eggshells around you."

"Don't you see?" She lowered her voice, and all she could think was that he needed help. How could she have dated him for over a year and not have known this about him? "Real lovers shouldn't have to walk on eggshells. They should expose their true selves."

"Bullshit. Okay, we don't have to go to Bali. We can talk it over and make a decision. And we can both set the date. Let's go back to the bar and forget this ever happened."

"Let go of me."

"Callie, I—"

"I'm sorry, Paul." She spoke through her gritted teeth. She wanted to take off her ring and give it to him. But to do that, he had to release her. "I don't love you."

"You'll learn to love me." Instead of releasing her, his grip tightened. "You need me, Callie."

"Let me go, or I'll scream."

His forehead furrowed, as if he couldn't connect to what he was saying. "Don't be silly, I'm not going to hurt you. I've never hurt a woman in my life. I just want to talk to you. After more than a year of dating me, don't I deserve that much?"

"You do, and I'm sorry, so sorry, I just..."

Voices rose from the smoking area, excitement in their tone, and she stared over Paul's shoulder.

Sam. Oh God, she didn't want him to see her like this.

"What are you looking at?" Paul twisted, and she could tell when he spotted Sam, his back and neck stiffening. "*Him?* The musician?" He turned back, and his eyebrows slashed together. "Don't tell me you have a crush on a *musician.*" He spat the last word.

"Sam and I went through school together." As she spoke, his complexion darkened. "We're old friends, and I'm happy for his success."

"If he's such a good friend, why didn't you want to come tonight? I had to practically drag you here."

"Maybe that should've told you something." Her eyebrows lowered. "Maybe I'm tired of you dragging me to do what I don't want to do."

"Why, you—" His voice rose, and so did his hand not holding her.

There was a shout from behind them, and she thought she heard the squeal of a cat, too. But she kept her eyes on Paul, the way she wouldn't take her eyes away from a dangerous animal about to attack.

Then his hand whipped toward her face, and she raised her free hand but knew it would be futile. In her peripheral was a blur of motion, but all she could focus on was that hand. It knocked her protective left hand away and slapped onto the side of her face, snapping her head to her right.

Making a small noise of pain and surprise, she lurched sideways, but she didn't fall, because he still held her wrist. As if she were his prisoner.

The next instant, he screamed; the blur she'd seen became a small, black panther lunging at his face. But it must have been a dream, because she'd never heard of panthers in central Wisconsin.

A black tail swished in her face, and Paul screamed again, releasing her. She reeled sideways, falling, her hand out. At the same time, she heard a man shouting.

Sam. He was coming to her rescue.

Too late, Sam. Nine years too late.

She tumbled to the sidewalk, landing on her knees, the palms of her hands on the concrete, stinging.

She was still on her knees, no time to scramble out of the way as Sam grabbed Paul's jacket and swung him into the wall of the knitting store. She could hear the thud of his back knocking into the red brick.

Good. I hope that hurts, you bastard.

"You fucking bully," Sam ground out. "I'll show you what it's like to hurt."

Urgency had her scrambling to her feet. She couldn't let him get into trouble because of her.

"Don't, Sam." She leapt at him, and when her knees hurt, she winced. She reached up to clasp his shoulder. "Please, Sam, don't do this."

"He hit you." He still gripped Paul's arm.

"It's over. Don't hurt your hands over this."

"I want to kill him."

"He's not worth it." She could hear the rawness in her voice, the begging. Damn it, did she have to pacify every man she knew? Did every woman have to do this?

She changed her stance, her hands on her hips, and glared. "Don't do anything stupid."

He looked at her, and as he did, Paul jerked away from him then shoved Sam with his freed hands, pushing him into her. She reached up to grab Sam's arm, so he wouldn't plow her down. But it was too late, and he stepped on the toe of her shoe.

As she was saying, "Ouch, ouch, ouch, ouch," Sam was turning and saying, "Oh, shit, I'm sorry. Damn it, I'm sorry." He peered over her head. "He's getting away."

A car door closed. Paul, she supposed.

Sam rushed toward the street, and she jumped after him, grabbing his waist and hanging on, a dead weight.

He twisted around, and only then did she release Sam so she could gaze into his eyes.

They stood there for a moment. Their breaths gasped as Paul's car squealed down the street away from them. Sam's head swiveled toward the street, and she entwined her arms around his waist to keep him from chasing after Paul's car.

"He's a coward, and he's gone," she said. "Good riddance."

Frustration flickered across his face, and she exhaled. It was over. God, what an asshole Paul had turned out to be. And how stupid was she to—

Something rubbed her ankle, and she looked down at the animal she'd thought was a panther. A cat looked up at her. It meowed again, this small cat who had attacked Paul so ferociously, protecting her.

"If no one owns you already, I'm going to keep you."

It meowed and rubbed its cheek against her leg. As if it were saying, *I'm yours. Take me home.* She tried to smile and realized she was shaking. She'd lost a fiancé, and maybe...just maybe...she'd gained a cat.

12

Sam's red-hot fury seeped out of him, but he was still tense as he turned to Callie. As he stared down at her, she stared back. It felt as if a door in his heart clicked open and charged emotions poured out.

Only his awareness of the onlookers kept him from putting his arms around her and holding her close. Nothing else. Just to show her he was there for her. Just to give her comfort.

Anything more would come later.

Her lips curved, one side up and one down, and she stepped back. "Hey, Sam."

"Hey, librarian," he said, too low for the others to hear.

Her eyes widened. Her lips opened. But she shook her head, as if shaking the words she wanted to say out of her mind. "You're my hero," she said clearly, her eyes darting to the onlookers, and an excited murmur rose behind him.

"Just doing my civic duty," he said.

"Cleaning out the trash?"

He wished to hell everyone on the sidewalk would disappear. But that only happened in dreams and graphic novels. "Something like that. Gotta admit, I'm surprised at you. I thought you had much better taste in men than that."

She laughed, and it sounded like the precursor to a cry. "I thought I did, too. Some people are better at hiding their true faces." She pushed her hair back from her face. "I'd better go home."

"What about the cat?" he asked.

As if understanding him, the cat meowed loudly. Callie bent and scooped it up. It meowed again, sounding like a complaint, but then it settled into her arms, leaning its head against her jacket, just above her heart.

Smart cat, he thought.

"The cat's my hero, too."

"It doesn't have a collar."

"It's a cat, city boy."

He laughed, and for that second, it felt to him like they were the old Sam and Callie.

"I'll take it home with me." Her fingers worked on the cat's neck. "Tomorrow, I'll call the humane society and see if anyone is missing this magnificent feline."

Another meow came from the cat.

"I think it's agreeing with you."

"Of course. It's a very smart cat. Aren't you?"

The cat gave another two meows, as if repeating her "of course," and they both laughed.

Despite her laughter, he could see the tension in her face.

"I'll drive you home."

"No, I have my car. I met Paul here. He was showing a house and..." She stopped, biting her lip.

"I'm glad you didn't drive with him," he said. "I'll walk you to your car."

She gave a short nod. As she led him down the street, he heard voices raised, people talking again—no doubt about them and what had just happened. A whiff of cigarette smoke came to him, then another, carrying in the cold air. Smoking as usual now that the excitement was over. Next to him, Callie's shoulders relaxed.

She stopped at a blue sedan parked in front of Sue's Bakery. Still holding the cat, she was about to walk around it to get inside when he asked, "What's your address?"

"I don't know if that's a good idea." She looked over her shoulder at him.

"Don't tell me you live with *him*."

Shaking her head, she turned around to face him. "No, and I'll be fine by myself."

"He might come over," Sam said. "Someone should stay with you all night."

"If there are any problems—which I very much doubt—I'll call the police."

"Do you really want to do that?"

Her lips flattened, her eyebrows lowered. "If I have to, I will."

He stared at her, and she stared right back. He exhaled loudly, the way men did sometimes to show their exasperation. "When did you get so stubborn?"

"I think I always was. Maybe you just didn't know it."

"That makes two of us. You don't want me to stay with you, that's fine. I'll just park my car in front of your place, bring a couple of my drums, and play them all night."

Her lips parted, and surprised laughter spurted out. She shrugged. "Idiot."

The cat meowed in three syllables, as if it were repeating the word.

"*Stubborn* idiot." He forced himself to remain standing apart from her. It had been a long time since he'd been called an idiot, but never by anyone looking at him with affection shining from her eyes.

She shook her head, but the affection lingered. "Don't you have to stay at your parents?"

"Not since I turned eighteen." He quirked an eyebrow. "What's your address? Either you tell me or I go in the bar and ask the crowd. Someone will know."

"You would, wouldn't you?" She groaned, not waiting for his answer. "You're not the same boy I knew."

"That's right. I'm a man." He left unsaid, *And you're a woman.*

She raised her left hand to pet the cat. "Remember my grandmother's house?"

He nodded. Every Christmas, her widowed grandmother put up a pink tree in the window.

When he'd asked Callie about it, she'd said her grandmother liked pink. That made sense to him, a boy who slept with three harmonicas in his bedroom because they made him feel good. As if they were all old friends of his.

"She lives in a condo in Arizona and gave me the house."

"Nice. I have to go back in and say good-bye." He jerked his chin toward the bar. "I'll be at your place in twenty minutes. Your ex has a key, doesn't he?"

"There was no reason to give him a key."

He felt a leap inside him. If he'd been engaged to her, or even her boyfriend, there would've been plenty of reasons to give him a key. "He might be waiting for you. Stay in the car until I get there."

"First, I'm not staying in the car until you come." She stepped back. "Second, I have to stop off and get cat supplies."

"At this time of the night?"

"The gas station store has an aisle of pet supplies." A wind gusted. She shivered and half turned. "It's open all night. I'm leaving now."

"Don't go inside if you see anything suspicious."

"Nothing suspicious will happen."

"Something already did."

"Paul won't do anything that will jeopardize his career."

"He already did." He gestured at the smokers. "There are witnesses."

"That was in the heat of the moment. He's not normally a man who gives in to the heat of the moment."

"He hit you. He did it once, and he could do it again. Or he could do something worse. So I'll be there soon. No arguments."

A frown creased her forehead. "Come in the alley way."

"I'll knock three times on the back door. If anyone knocks more or less, don't even look outside the door."

"You're crazy." Her laugh sounded nervous and excited. She stepped around the car. "I have to go now."

"I'm not kidding. If it's not three times, don't answer it unless you have a gun."

"It won't be Paul. I know him."

"Did you know he was an asshole?"

"He hates to look foolish. He'll blame me for what happened. He won't be back."

"If he doesn't fight for you, he's a fool."

She stared at him over the trunk of her car. "If that's true, that makes you a fool."

"I know." And he turned and headed toward the bar, the music, the smokers, and thought that it didn't make him a fool once.

It made him a fool twice.

* * *

At the gas station with the small mart, she worried that if she opened the door, the cat might rush out and run away. It was small and quick, and she was bigger and slower. She told the cat she was going in to get her food. The cat meowed, as if it understood. Keeping her gaze on it, she slid out, hardly daring to breathe, but the cat remained in the passenger seat, its unblinking green eyes never leaving her face.

"I'm coming back," she said.

The cat meowed, as it telling her it understood her. Of course, that couldn't be true, but her mind seemed to be speeding in circles. Too much had happened, and she didn't know what any of it meant, except that she had lost a fiancé—and good riddance to that—and she might have gained a cat. And as for Sam...

Her heartbeat quickened, and she hurried into the small store, rushing past the candy aisles that always tempted her, and to the less popular pet aisle. A few minutes later, she dumped the heavy litter bag on the checkout counter where some guy who looked like he was in his teens was buying a gallon of ice cream. As he told the clerk it was for his pregnant girlfriend, Callie hurried back for the litter pan.

There was no cat food. A middle-aged woman who came in for chocolate and to pay for her gas told her that strained baby food in chicken or beef was healthier than cat food. Callie bought a half dozen jars then gave into temptation and bought a bag of kettle corn and a dark chocolate candy bar. After all, dark chocolate was brain food.

Back in the car, the cat waited for her calmly in its seat, once again not trying to get out. As if it knew her.

She laughed at herself. In a night that was going crazy, that was one more crazy thing.

And she realized for the first time, it was a full moon night.

She was not surprised.

Of course, Paul wasn't waiting for her when she reached home. He was probably doing damage control already. Calling friends and relatives to put his spin on what had happened, putting her in a bad light.

She felt bad, knowing she was in the wrong.

She should never have said yes. She'd had doubts, and she'd ignored them.

"When should a girl stop waiting for Mr. Right?" she asked the cat, setting it on her wooden kitchen floor. "When should she settle for Mr. Good Enough?"

Staring at her, the black cat spoke in a series of meows and mrews, in what sounded like whole sentences, and at least a few paragraphs.

"I wish I knew what you're saying," she said. "I'm sure it's very sound advice."

She made two more trips to the detached garage, the back light on. Hurrying the whole time, just in case Sam's worries were right. Of course, she knew they weren't, but still, she breathed with relief when the door was safely locked behind her. She just wasn't the kind of person who normally attracted violence. She was kind of...boring.

Until tonight.

She put a hand to the side of her face. It didn't feel sore. Maybe she wouldn't get a bruise that she'd have to cover up with makeup.

The phone rang, her parents' number showing on the display. Of course, they'd heard what happened. Probably everyone she knew had heard by now. Though she didn't know everyone in Eagleton, she knew a lot of people, and they knew her.

She put the phone to her ear, and both of her parents, on different extensions in their house, spoke at once. Callie assured them she was fine and added that her engagement was off. Her mother said it was good, because her father was threatening to call the police on Paul for hitting her.

Wincing, Callie said it wasn't necessary. "Did anyone tell you about the Ninja cat I picked up?"

That changed the conversation. As she petted the cat, she told her parents how smart it was, as well as brave.

"Sounds like a dog," her dad said.

The cat meowed, as if it agreed, though Callie was sure that if the cat understood her father, it would be loudly objecting.

"Don't get too attached before you know for sure no one else wants her," her mother said. "You have such a soft heart."

"Honey," her dad said, "it's an attack cat. I hope no one else claims it. She could use a cat like that, especially now that we know what Paul is like." His voice roughened. "I'm going to drive over to your place with your grandpa's twenty-two. Just in case he comes over there."

"Dad!" She sat up. "I don't want a loaded gun in the house. Besides, the deadlocks are on. There's nothing to worry about. And I have the cat to protect me."

Her mother protested, too, saying he would end up in jail. Her dad grumpily gave in, but he warned her to sleep with her cell phone next to her.

She thought she might be sleeping with something warmer and bigger than a cell phone. Breathing, too. But some things she didn't share with her parents. "He won't try anything. If something bad happened to me, he'd be the first suspect."

"And he's too selfish for that," her mom said with a spitefulness unusual for her.

They hung up, and Callie thought about the sleeping thing—okay, the making love thing. She hurried to the bathroom to brush her teeth. Her heart beating quickly, she looked at herself in the mirror. Though some men called her pretty or even beautiful, she knew they were hoping they'd get lucky. Of course, they thought *she* was getting lucky, too.

For the first time since she was eighteen, she wondered if she would get lucky.

Not that she expected fireworks. That just didn't happen to her. But that human connection and joining was something to be treasured. And it led to children, which she wanted in the not-too-far future. It was the reason she'd gotten engaged to a man she didn't love.

She wasn't going to do that again. But tonight she didn't expect anything. She just hoped for...something more. Hoped very hard.

One children's book that she loved said that if you hoped hard enough, it would come true.

She didn't believe that hoping was enough. But she did believe it was a start.

Headlights beamed into the yard, a car pulling up next to the garage.

The cat made a noise that sounded like a growl, and Callie rinsed out her mouth and her toothbrush then pushed up her hair. Feeling lightheaded, she hurried to the door to let in her first love. Not her last. Her last love had had four legs, a wagging tail, and floppy ears.

It was going to be hard for any man to top that.

13

"Hey." Sam stood inside Callie's kitchen. The ex wasn't there, just him and Callie and the cat. Callie had asked for his jacket. Now, if only she'd say, *"And your sweater, and your jeans, and your underwear, and your shoes, and your socks."* Or *"Keep your socks on but take off everything else"* would work, too.

None of those words came from her mouth, so he stood there like a doofus and tried to look cool. After all, he was a cool guy—a musician. With a Grammy! And she was a librarian. A nerd, right?

But she grinned as if she was happy to see him. As if they were just Callie and Sam, all grown up. And none of that library and Grammy stuff mattered.

She hung his jacket up instead of throwing it on the chair, and it made him smile, because that was just like her. Finally he tugged his stare away and nodded at the black cat. "I'm glad the attack cat is here with you."

She laughed, and just like the first time he'd heard her laugh, it was still the best sound he'd heard.

"Did I ever tell you that your laugh sounds like sunshine?" he asked.

"Never." She beamed at him. She'd changed her

shoes for slippers, and she looked closer to a teenager than twenty-seven, just a few months younger than him.

"It probably sounded too dorky. Even when I was four years old."

"My mom remembers me telling her that you made it across the bars with the rope handles at recess. Apparently, I was very impressed."

He'd felt happiness often in the past nine years. A lot of good things had happened since he'd last seen her. And a lot of shitty things had happened. There'd been contract hassles, bounced checks, and threats of lawsuits. They'd lost one label, and another label had picked them up. There'd been two changes of front men in their band, until he and Rick said the hell with it and went with just Rick. And then Justen joined them, and it was like joining honey with strawberry jam.

And then there'd been the Grammys. That had felt like the fans and the industry were all saying, *You're good. We love you.*

They knew it was temporary, but, hot damn, it was like God giving them a nudge and a hug.

But out of all that, nothing made him as happy as standing in Callie's kitchen that smelled like lemons and hearing her laughter and seeing her face light up.

"I know I said I was coming here to guard you," he said.

"So you did." She stood still, her expression

turning serious.

"But that wasn't the real reason."

"I was hoping it wasn't." Though her lips didn't smile, her eyes were bright.

"Do you mind if I kiss you?" he asked.

"I'll only mind if you don't do a lot more than that," she said.

Joy roared up inside him as he took one step toward her. She was laughing again, his favorite sound in the world, but he still put his mouth over hers, and she still laughed into his mouth.

* * *

Her laughter caught in her throat.

She was instantly on fire, as if his lips had been the match, his kiss the fuel. Their bodies pressed together, and she could tell he had the same reaction, as if the wildfire blazed over him, too.

Still kissing her, he picked her up and set her on the wooden table. His arms around her, he gently sucked her lower lip into his mouth.

She gripped his upper arms tightly. She was melting. Her legs parted, and he fitted snugly between them. The pressure sent a thrill through her. She made a mewling noise. An orgasm, she thought, even as she clung to him, rocking on the table. For the first time in her twenty-seven years, she was having an orgasm with a man, both of them fully clothed and not touching below their necks.

She wrapped her legs around his butt. She didn't know why this was happening now, but it happened again. And again. As if the gates of heaven had opened up and let her in, with a chorus of angels singing "Hallelujah."

"Oh, Jesus," he said, his voice strangled. "Oh, Jesus."

Moaning, she held back another mew. She had to think. One of them had to. Right now, the coolest head in the house belonged to the cat.

She pulled back and realized she was panting. "We should take our clothes off."

Using his lips, he'd pushed down the neckline of her top as far as it would go, just an inch or two. "I don't want to let you go," he murmured. "I'm on fire for you."

She put up her hands and shoved her open palms against his shoulders so he finally let go of her. She was cold instantly. Missing him instantly. Being mere inches from him was too far.

Still on the table, she whipped off her top.

He ripped his shirt off, and buttons popped. The ridiculous thought came into her mind that buttons really did fly off. She'd seen it happen in films and on TV but had never believed it.

She'd begun to wonder if an orgasm was a myth, too. As if everyone lied about it. But right now, her body was one small orgasm after another, with a big orgasm about to happen.

And she didn't plan to delay it.

His shoes and socks were off already, and he was working on his pants.

She slid off the table in order to pull her pants off. It was hard because he shed his first, and her hands tingled, her whole body tingled, and she just wanted to get on her knees and start worshiping him.

At eighteen, he'd been good-looking. At twenty-seven, his body was even better, his muscles more defined, and he had the six-pack thing going on.

She wanted to kiss and lick every muscle. Every inch of skin.

While he grabbed a condom from his wallet to cover up a good number of inches of that skin, she hurried to pull off her panties and leave them on the floor with a wince at her messiness.

Then he was lifting her into his arms, as if she weighed as little as the cat, when she was a normal-sized woman whose best form of exercise was bending and reaching to put library books away.

He turned to the living room, and she laughed with giddiness. With lightness.

"What's funny?" he asked.

"I'm love-shot."

"That makes two of us. Where's your bedroom?"

"Upstairs. I can walk."

"Later." He dropped her on her couch.

She bounced and laughed again.

Everything was funny.

Everything was sexy.

Everything was wonderful.

Then he was on top of her and between her legs. Immediately, the fire shot through her again. This time she screamed, a thin, reedy, and glorious sound as her body clenched and unclenched. Amazing and wonderful.

He made grunting noises on top of her and then an "ah, ah, ah" chant that turned her on even more, and she hung on tightly, small animal sounds coming from her throat. He raised his head, the cords in his neck sticking out, and he shuddered above her and inside her while she pushed tightly around him.

Then it was over, and he shook as he lay on her while she was splayed out on the couch. His heart thundered against her chest, and her own thundered back. Inside her, he was still contracting—like earthquake aftershocks.

She felt satiated. Wiped out. Fulfilled. All the best words she could think of, except she wasn't thinking much at all. She was just...happy.

They stayed like that until she shivered, the warm sweat on their bodies cooling. He pushed up, his chest off of her but their lower bodies still connected.

"I feel like a train ran me over," he said.

"You, too? I thought it was just me." She made a face, because it was going to sound funny, but she wanted to know. "Is it like this for you every time?"

"Not like this. This was..."

"Magic." She felt a big smile take over her face. "It's a first for me. First orgasm. I think I made up for all the other times."

"You're kidding? The other time we did it—"

"Nope." She made an apologetic face. "I did enjoy it."

"It was your first time. It had to hurt."

"Just a bit of discomfort. And then I did like it." She pushed up on her elbows. "But tonight... It was...incredible. Now I get what all the songs are about. The reason people do stupid things for love."

He pulled out of her and rolled off her and the couch, standing on the blue-and-cream area carpet. "You can be stupid with me anytime you want. And I'll be just as stupid right back."

She got up and saw that, incredibly, inside his condom that didn't seem to fit right anymore, his penis was lengthening and thickening again.

She moaned, and she could hear the tiredness in her moan...and she could hear the excitement.

"How do you get so much stamina?" she asked. "You just toured for seven months."

"You're keeping track of me?" He grinned.

"Yep." She grinned back. "Not all the time. When I have trouble sleeping, I've sometimes looked you up. I'm so happy for you."

"It's what I want to do with my life." He shrugged. "I don't know what I'd do without music.

Music saved me."

He spoke simply, as if it were a fact, but in her mind, she saw the sad and angry face of the six-year-old boy who'd broken up with her. The boy who'd been convinced he was stupid.

A wordless sound of compassion came out of her mouth, and she stepped up to him, her arms out. He grasped both her forearms, stopping her inches away. "Don't feel sorry for me. It's all good." He gazed at her, his eyebrows slanted down, and she saw the truth in his eyes. "Everything that happened was good. It made me concentrate on my music, my drumming. Music was the one thing I did well, and I poured my heart into it."

She jerked her right arm out of his grip then put a hand on her hip and looked pointedly down his body. When she gazed upward, she said, "It's not pity I'm feeling for you now."

His eyes warmed. "It's not pity I'm feeling for you, either. I'll need another condom."

"How do you do it?" She gestured at his growing erection. "I wouldn't call myself an expert, but I'm pretty sure most men aren't ready for a second round so quickly."

"Only with you."

She laughed and shook her head. She wanted to believe him...but she was a librarian, and she hadn't met one yet who was stupid. "You must take care of yourself when you tour."

"It's important to take care of myself. I feel

better when I keep fit. I play better, too."

"You look like you keep fit."

"You look pretty good, too." His voice lowered, reminding her of warm maple syrup.

"I do yoga," she said.

"Meditation? It's good for the library brain?"

"It's good for any brain. But it also makes me flexible." She flushed. Here she was, standing naked in front of him after making love to him, telling him how flexible her body was.

"I'm all for flexibility," he said.

"I'll be happy to show you some of my moves." She grinned.

"It's not just my body's fitness that makes me ready for you so soon."

"What else?"

"Deprivation."

She lifted her eyebrow. "Of sexual partners? Seriously?"

"Deprivation of *you*. I don't think I'll ever get enough of you."

Another flush warmed her. Happiness, she thought. Pure happiness.

Or else it was pure bullshit.

For tonight, she thought, she would believe he was telling the truth.

"Then let's both get some right now. This time, can we do it in the bed?"

She put out her hand, and he took it. Together, they started for the stairs.

14

He left the house two hours later, while she was sleeping. He did it for her, backing out of her alley with his lights off, steering onto the street before turning them on. Making sure no one saw him leave.

It was enough that people had witnessed the public breakup between her and the asshole. In a city this small, it wouldn't do the reputation of Eagleton's purchasing librarian any good if it were known that she'd been sleeping with the drummer of a band that sang about sex, love, cheating, drinking, and leaving. Especially one that had won a Grammy with its song about having sex with a librarian.

A lot of people had crammed into his parents' bar last night to celebrate with Rick and him. But that wouldn't stop the library board's disapproval if they got news of what she and he had done. Throwing his dyslexia into the mix would double their disapproval. Through the years, he'd run into quite a few people who didn't believe in dyslexia. Who thought he was faking his dyslexia. Who thought he was stupid.

He didn't give a damn what they thought about him. But what they thought about Callie mattered.

He was lucky he'd had Rick all these years. He

counted on Rick to read his contracts and anything else he needed. In return, he was the one who told Rick when a note was wrong, or when a riff went on too long or too short. Rick had an ear, but Sam had an ear quadrupled. Justen had once said that God was compensating for him not being able to read.

He wasn't sure himself what he thought about God or if he was convinced there was one. If there was, he had a hell of a twisted sense of humor, and when Sam died and went up to heaven, he had a lot of questions to ask the big guy.

Though if God suddenly appeared right now, right this moment, he would just grin and thank him.

Tonight had been his own slice of heaven. His problem was that now he wanted the whole cake.

* * *

Her eyes open, Callie listened to the small rumble of Sam's engine. In the daytime, she wouldn't hear it, but in the clear, frosty night, it came to her softly. Then the sound grew quieter and, in a moment, it was gone. *He* was gone. Driving away from her.

It felt as if happiness was driving away from her.

She closed her eyes and told herself not to be silly.

Instead she stretched, a long, luxurious stretch.

Her body felt languid. Some days it was better to listen to her body instead of her mind. As for that worry in her mind that he would leave her heartbroken again, she would close it, like it was a book in the library that she didn't want to read, then put it away, out of her sight.

There was a thud on her bed, the mattress dipping. A meow sang out, and her eyes snapped open to soft rays of moonlight. The next second, a soft-furred animal was rubbing its cheek against her jaw.

She reached up to pet the silky fur. Already she felt affection for the cat and hoped no one claimed it.

The cat curled up on her side, and she rubbed her nose against the soft fur. A cat would never take the place of Magic, but at least she wouldn't be alone for the rest of the night.

After that... She exhaled. Closing the thoughts from her mind, she petted the humming cat and just felt.

15

Sam's mom waited in the kitchen for him when he shuffled in, yawning, not fully awake. "Hey, Mom." He felt good this morning. The same way a machine might feel when a missing piece was found and restored.

Callie was his missing piece.

There was silence as he headed toward the fridge. Cold silence. By the time he opened the door, he admitted to himself that the chill in the air was more frigid than the temperature in the refrigerator.

All these years away from his mom, and she still knew how to dim a great after-sex glow. Even an amazing after-sex glow.

He took out the orange juice container, stepping to the counter and screwing off the plastic cap. He knew better than to drink it in front of the open fridge door with his mom in the same room.

As he lifted it to his mouth, she said, "You aren't drinking it out of the bottle, are you?"

The razor edge to her tone that said if-you-do-I'll-hurt-you made him lower the container and take out a glass. He'd been on the road for a while and had forgotten about his mother's idiosyncrasies.

"No." He held up the glass, as if that had been

his plan all along.

Her lips pressed together. She wasn't buying it. His mom didn't look bad for her age. She'd been young when she'd had him, only nineteen, six months after she and his dad had married. Neither she nor his dad had let their mistakes stop them from telling him what he should do. They thought it gave them the right to say they knew what they were talking about.

"Where were you last night?" she asked.

"Mom, I'm twenty-seven. I don't have to answer these questions."

"You were with Callie, weren't you?"

He cocked an eyebrow at her. Not answering.

She slumped into her chair. "I thought so." Her mouth remained stern. "I saw the way you looked at each other. Jesus, if you were two dogs, you would've been going at it in the middle of the dance floor."

Jeez. Only his mother would say something like that. "Hey, Mom, if you were any blunter, you'd be hitting my head with a hammer."

"Don't give me any ideas."

"Okay, then, with a bag of marshmallows."

"Real funny. I'll stick with the hammer."

"Mom, I *like* Callie."

"I like her, too." His mom crossed her arms and gave him the laser-beam look that she did so well. It was too bad they didn't have a cat like the one Callie had saved. His mom could've used her laser-eyes on dark nights for the cat to chase, as they would no doubt show up as two pinpoints of red light.

He set the glass on the counter. "I love her."

Her expression didn't soften; her laser gaze didn't waver. "Are you going to ask her to marry you?"

He didn't answer. He wasn't ten anymore.

"You're not going to stay in Eagleton, are you?"

He didn't want to answer her. He didn't want to think about leaving Callie. Just the thought of it felt like a stone in his chest.

"I can't stay."

Her eyebrow lifted, and the stone in his chest got heavier.

"We have to tour. We've finally made it, and we have to get in front of as many faces as we can. And somehow during that time, we have to make another album."

"That's what I thought. You can't sit on your laurels."

"Or my Grammy." He forced a grin, and she didn't smile back. She didn't look mad anymore, either. She just looked...older. Sadder. Her shoulders sagged as if she'd been carrying a heavy load.

As if she felt the same heavy stone in her chest that he did.

"You toured eleven months out of twelve the last few years," she said.

He tensed. He looked at the table with the salt and pepper containers and the napkin holder that looked like a guitar on one side and a banjo on the other. He thought about sitting and pretending not to hear her. But it wouldn't stop her. When Brenda Krushing made up her mind to do something, she was a force of nature. And not the mild, sunny side of nature, either. She could be mean and dark and create a hell of a storm.

He glanced up. "Your point is?"

"You know my point. She won't tour with you, and you'll cheat on her."

"You're wrong. I won't."

"You're a guy." Her voice was flat.

"Not every guy cheats. Are you saying Dad cheated? I don't believe that."

"I don't give him the chance to cheat. Why do you think I work with him? Why do you think I learned how to play the guitar?"

"Jesus, Mom. This is more than I want to know about you and Dad."

"Then you shouldn't have brought it up. My dad cheated, my granddad cheated, my brothers cheated." She shrugged. "I come from a long line of cheating men. I wasn't about to go through what my mom and grandma went through."

He pushed his fingers through his hair. *Grandpa? Uncle Roger and Uncle Andy?*

Some things he didn't want to know. From now on, every time he'd look at them, he'd respect them a little less.

"I'm sorry it was so tough for you. But I won't cheat. I just won't. I love her. I've always loved her."

"She's special, I know. But she's also the one who got away. Isn't that what this is about?"

He stood straight. "Not anything near." His voice was harsh. "You aren't listening to me. Callie and I are reconnecting, and anything that needs to be worked out, we'll do it. We're adults and don't need any advice from you. Don't worry, I don't plan on hurting her."

Her eyes changed, looking weepy without tears, and the lines on each side of her mouth softened. "Maybe it's not her I'm worried about. Maybe it's you."

"When did you turn this into a doomsday story?" He scowled at her. "You're like Chicken Little, always looking at the sky, afraid it will fall down on you."

"I worry because I love you. I remember what you were like as a kid before you were diagnosed. You didn't know what was going on." Her forehead furrowed. "None of us knew why you couldn't read when you tried so hard. You became angry and defensive. But you stuck through it, and now look at where you are." She swept her arm out.

"I'm in the kitchen with you," he snapped. "That's where I am."

Tears sprang up in her eyes, and he immediately felt like a piece of shit. He mentally counted the days he'd be here. Six more and he'd be free again. On the road, which he'd been so glad to get off of just a few days ago.

Then it hit him. He'd be away from his mom...and he'd also be away from Callie.

His stomach twisted. How could he have forgotten? Even for a second?

"Maybe she can tour with me," he said.

"Honey." His mom shook her head. "She's lucky to have gotten a job in the library. Shirley Jamison stayed on at the library for an extra two years so they could hire her to take over her position." She held out her hand, her palm a foot from his face, to stop him from talking. "They're lucky to have her, I know. And so do they. But it helped that she was a native, and she and her family went to the same church as half the library board. And that Shirley was a good friend of her grandmother's."

"They are lucky to have her."

"Even so, there's no way you can have an affair with Callie without some judgmental asshole finding out and getting pissy about it."

This time he kept his mouth shut.

"And if you're thinking she'll quit her job and travel with you, think again. She won't leave her mother."

"You know, Mom." He stepped past her, toward the hall door that led to the staircase downstairs. "This is a lousy way to wake up."

Her voice followed him, dripping with sarcasm.

"So sorry you had to wake up to the naked truth from your mother. I'm sure you'd much rather be woken up like Callie's mother, with your immune system attacking your nerve endings and spinal cord, clenching your teeth tightly to keep from screaming in agony."

He wanted to stomp away from her, but he wasn't an angry kid anymore who couldn't read. Now he was an adult, and he couldn't stomp out of the tough parts of life, though he sure the hell wanted to. He turned, hunching, feeling a new weight on his shoulders. "She's that bad now?"

"The last time her parents were here, Travis said Lydia was taking something experimental that seemed to be helping a bit."

He stood still. As irritating as his mom was right now, getting into his business, she was still his mom, and he was grateful for her.

"Mom, if you were sick, I wouldn't want to leave you, either."

Her face colored. "If I were sick," she said, sounding younger than a moment ago, "I'd tell you to go. I wouldn't need you hovering over me, getting in my way." She put her hands on her hips. "What are you going to do?"

He didn't answer right away, his head down, thinking hard as she remained silent. When he was ready, he raised his head. "Whatever is best for her, that's what I'm going to do."

16

Callie knew her mom would be worrying. Morning sunlight streamed into her parents' kitchen, and one look at the frown on her mother's still-beautiful face told her she was right to drive over.

Standing by the kitchen table, Lydia held out her arms. Callie closed her eyes and let her mother enfold her in a hug.

They stayed like that for a long moment before pulling away. "Coffee?" her mom asked.

"I'll get it," Callie said. If they were going to talk about last night, she needed coffee.

When she sat, her mom put her hand on top of hers. Her mom's fingers were long and thin, the blue veins on the back of her hand making it look skeleton-like.

"I'm just happy you found out Paul's true self before you married him," her mom said.

"Me, too. But that's not all that happened." She hadn't planned on saying anything, but she wanted to see her mother smile. Wanted her to feel happy—the way she did. Even if it was like a weather report: *Happy with a touch of sad.*

"You won the lottery?" Her mom picked up her coffee cup.

Callie laughed, shaking her head.

"*People Magazine* called," Lydia said. "They're writing an article on the 'Most Beautiful Librarians,' and you're number one."

Callie slapped her knees with laughter. People felt sorry for her that her mother was sick, but she felt sorry for them for not having a mother who gave them so much love. Unconditional. Lydia never asked anything of Callie or even expected it. Callie thought that was why she wanted to give so much. Her mother was an example of the kind of woman she wanted to be.

"No, I'm in love."

Her mother's smile never faltered, but her eyes changed, emotions flickering across her face so swiftly that Callie couldn't read them. "That's wonderful. Darling, I'm so happy for you. Not Paul, I know. Who's the lucky man?"

"You know him already."

Her mother stilled again, and for a second, she looked incandescent, as if she were lit from the inside. "Sam Krushing, right?"

"How did you guess?"

Lydia's slender fingers curved over Callie's head. Her blue eyes were giving blessings to Callie. "You never stopped loving him."

"You can't mean that. That was ages ago."

"You never stopped," she repeated.

Callie shook her head. "I did. I stopped when we got Magic. I transferred all that love to him."

"No, you didn't. You loved Magic. Who wouldn't

love him? But it didn't take the place of loving Sam. You don't have a limited amount of love. Real love has no limits."

"I was six." She heard the finality in her voice and didn't even know why she was arguing. She'd worried that her mother would be concerned. That she would say it was impossible. It was wrong. That it wasn't really love. That when Sam left, the love would leave, too.

Instead her mother was saying she knew it all along.

"You were four when you fell in love with him." Her mom's smile didn't dip, not in her eyes or on her lips, but she pulled back her hand. "How many boys did you love since Sam? And don't say Paul. Your dad and I always knew you were settling."

"I hadn't met the right one yet."

"I think you did meet the right one." Lydia's forehead wrinkled. "Why are you arguing about it? Are you afraid he doesn't feel the same way?" Her voice softened. "He'd be a fool not to feel the same way."

"I think he does."

"But you're not sure?"

"I'm sure." But her voice shook a bit, and she wondered what that meant.

Perhaps because he'd broken her heart once. Her heart had mended, but the crack was still there. This time around, it was harder to believe he felt the same way about her. Harder to push away the doubts.

If it happened once, it could happen again.

"Giving your heart to a man can be scary," her mother said, as if she could read her mind.

"You're so wise."

"I am that." Her smile was tender, a mix of sadness and light. "When you love someone, there's always a chance that he might not love you as much as you love him."

Callie stood. A tremor was starting inside her. A lot different from last night's tremors when she was making love with Sam. Those wonderful, wonderful tremors.

"He can't stay here," Callie said. "He's on the road most of the time."

"Go with him."

"And do what? The band travels together in a bus. I could do that for a week or two. Maybe three. But not much longer than that. I have my job."

"Is your job that important to you? More important than Sam?"

The tremor was still inside her, and she clenched her hands to stop it. "I like my job. I don't know that I'd like traveling in a bus for months. In fact, I'm pretty sure I wouldn't." She frowned. "And I don't think the other band members would like it, either. Besides, I might have a cat now."

"The one who protected you last night?"

Callie nodded. "She's not really mine. I still have to call to see if anyone is looking for her. I hope no one is."

Her mother stood. She didn't jump up, but she didn't need to keep a hand on the table, either. Callie's tremors stopped. That was...the best.

"You're not staying because of me?" her mom asked. "Because I would hate that."

"I'm staying for all the other reasons. And you know what, Mom? He hasn't asked me to do anything. He hasn't mentioned the future, and neither have I." She turned toward the door. "I have to go to work."

"Just swear to me..."

The intensity in her mom's tone made her turn back. For once, Lydia wasn't smiling, Her blue eyes fixed on Callie's face, as if she was trying to catch every nuance. Every flicker of her eye. Every contraction of her muscles. She wanted to see the truth.

Callie inhaled sharply, studying her mom. Only forty-eight, her hair had turned prematurely white, but her face was unlined, her skin still soft, her lips still full.

Still beautiful, her dad said, and Callie agreed. She didn't look like a person with a debilitating illness. But looks didn't always tell the truth.

"Swear that you won't stay because of me."

Callie sucked in her lower lip, biting it.

"Swear," her mom repeated. "I want you to swear."

"Mom, he hasn't asked me to do anything. And I

honestly don't know if I would."

"That's not what I'm asking. If there's any opportunity for happiness, with or without Sam, I want you to take it. Swear that you will."

Tears warmed Callie's eyes, and she blinked them back. "I want to say yes, but I don't know..." She didn't say it, but the unsaid words hung in the air. *I don't know if the improvement in your health will last. I don't know if you'll develop symptoms that will make you drop out of the testing program, and you'll regress back to where you started. I don't know anything for sure.*

"Know this," her mother said firmly. "If you stay because of me, it would sadden me. If you lose any opportunity for happiness because of me, I would hate it. I would just...hate it."

"But, Mom, I don't know."

"No one knows." Her mother spoke softly, and she even smiled, but that didn't take away from the strength of her words. "Anything can happen, and sometimes it does and it's good, and sometimes something better happens. You know what something better is?"

She shook her head. "Something better can be a lot of things."

"Yes. It could be love. True love. That's what I have with your dad. And I don't know how it happened, but I think you found your true love when you were four, and that's the reason you never fell in love again."

Callie shivered, because she thought the same thing. As if there were a cosmic joke, giving a woman who loved books a true love who couldn't read. And to top it off, he traveled and she was a homebody.

What next?

She shivered harder. If there was any *next,* she didn't want to know.

"Mom. If he asks, I won't say no because of you."

"You swear?"

She raised her right hand, making a pledge. "I swear."

"Good." Her mom nodded firmly. "Good."

Callie reached forward, hugged and kissed her, then hurried out of the house, feeling unsettled. If Sam asked her to leave Eagleton, she couldn't use her mother as an excuse to stay...and that scared her more than Paul's anger last night. What kind of life would she have with him?

And what kind of life would she have without him?

Anything she did would take away something else, and her problem was that, like most people, she wanted it all. Wanted it so much, it was an ache in her heart.

And like most people, she couldn't have it all. Sooner or later, she'd have to make decisions, and just hope to hell she was making the right one.

17

Sam parked in front of Callie's house. The light was dimming, but people could see his mother's black Jeep easily. It felt odd having a platinum album and still driving his mother's car, but that was how family worked. He and Rick had driven together from the Minneapolis-St. Paul Airport. Since Rick's mom needed her car for work, Rick kept the rental and Sam used his mom's car. It didn't make sense to spend money on another rental when he'd be here for less than a week.

At his heart, he had the Midwestern frugality. Rick, too. In this business, it's what had gotten them this far.

On the charts.

And here. To Callie's house.

He grabbed the square, flat, great-smelling box from the passenger seat then headed toward Callie's house, excitement simmering inside him.

Yesterday, he'd parked in the back. Like a thief. Then he'd come in through the back door. Like a sneak. Yesterday, he was a guy who'd come to get lucky.

Today, he wanted more.

The door opened, and she beamed at him.

It felt like the sun was shining down on him instead of the first beams from the moon. He grinned back at her.

"Do you remember our first date?" he asked.

"On the playground? You wanted me to watch your athletic prowess?"

"And you did. I was like a chimpanzee, showing off for the lady chimpanzee."

"You should put that in your next record. I'm sure your female fans would love to be compared to lady chimpanzees as much I do."

"Good idea. I'll run it by the band." He grinned. He felt alive-plus with her. As if extra brain cells were firing and his skin had thinned, so he felt every breath she exhaled; every move she made.

He held up the box. "Offerings for a goddess."

She stepped back, and he stepped inside. "It's only goddess material if it has extra olives and mushrooms," she said.

"It does. My dad said it's your favorite." He handed her the pizza then took off his jacket and grimaced. "It's weird that my father knows more about my girlfriend than I do."

Hanging up his jacket in the hall closet, he felt silence behind him. No movement, no talk, nothing.

He turned around slowly, not knowing what he'd said that changed the atmosphere. This boy-girl stuff had been easier when he was four. You invited a girl to see you perform on the playground equipment at recess. And if you really liked her at lunch, you gave her one of the two cookies your mom put in your backpack. And if she liked you, she gave you her apple.

Now it was more complicated. And he meant *right now*, because right now was when he was looking at her, and she wasn't smiling, she wasn't frowning. She just stood in the small front hall as if she'd been frozen, her eyes wide, her eyebrows raised.

"Girlfriend?" she asked.

"I'm not sure what you'd call us." He frowned. "We matter. It's not just about sex."

"It's not?" She blinked. "I guess that's good. Considering I'm not that great in bed, I'm glad that it's not just sex."

He laughed low in his throat. "You're way off."

"I am?" Her lips parted, her eyes watched his eyes.

He didn't know if this was another benefit of his abnormal brain, but he could hear the sparks crackle in the air. He could feel currents of warm air touching him.

Or maybe he was just nuts.

"Sex isn't about experience," he said, "it's about emotion."

"Oh yeah?" Her blue eyes lit up, and the corners of her lips curled up, forming a smile of a woman who knew how much she was wanted.

It was more than confidence, he thought. It was Wonder Woman's invisible golden lariat wrapping around him, pulling him to her.

He stepped toward her, because who could resist the golden lariat? Not him. And who would want to run away from the lariat? Not him. Never him.

She could wrap him up and tie him down, and she'd never hear one word of complaint.

"I don't think we need this, do we?" He took the box out of her hands. She laughed again, low and shivery. No music could match it. It still sounded like sunlight to him, if sunlight had a voice. It warmed him, whispering of pleasures to come.

"You're not hungry?" she asked.

"I'm very hungry." He brushed his gaze up and down her body in her jeans and red Badgers sweatshirt. "But not for food."

She took the pizza back from him and started to walk away. He had the "oh shit" drop in his belly that she was going to ignore the fireworks between them. That she wanted to eat the pizza and maybe chat.

He straightened. It wouldn't be the first time he'd thought he was in the same rhythm with a woman only to find out he wasn't even playing the same tune. Usually, he shrugged it off. But this time, it was a sharp note inside his chest.

Then she looked behind her, and now she was grinning. "I'll put this on the counter. We can work up an appetite."

The sharp note smoothed, and it was all mellow and all good. Sexy blues notes played inside him, humming through his blood stream. And all he could do was grin back and follow her. Just like in kindergarten...only better. Much, much better as anticipation banged its own magic inside his head, loud and heavy and so wonderful it made him want to climb on top of the roof and shout her name up to the skies.

A crazy man shouting about his crazy, sexy love.

* * *

They closed the door on the cat, but she knew what they were doing. Animals were born knowing about this. When the need came upon them, they satisfied it quickly and thoroughly.

Humans took a lot longer than was necessary.

Soft laughter and the hums and squeals and even smells came from the bedroom.

The laughter stopped, replaced by moans and heavy breathing. Sometimes a high, keening pitch.

The scents wafting toward her turned darker and heavier. The scent of mating.

Then the sounds changed to mews and grunts.

Assured that Callie was all right, the cat padded downstairs.

She moved to the front of the house since the bedroom was in the back. Curling on the couch, she closed her eyes to nap.

Right now, Callie didn't need her. When Callie did, she would be there for her.

18

Sam felt like he could conquer the world. He grinned while they sat at the kitchen table and ate their warmed-up pizza, and she beamed back at him. He was on his fourth piece when the call came. He took his phone off his belt and glanced down at it, ready to turn it off, and saw the image on his screen.

"It's Rick," he said.

"Answer it."

"I'll turn it off after this," he said, lifting it to his ear then pressing Talk.

"It's started again," Rick said.

"What started again?"

"Your stalker."

"Shit. Well, if she doesn't—"

"Barney called. She posted on our website this afternoon. She said she's coming to Eagleton to watch you."

He froze.

"And if she finds you with another woman, she's going to hurt her."

"Shit."

"Yeah. I told Barney to call Security."

"Shit."

"Is that all you can say?"

"Right now? Yeah."

"You with Callie now?"

"Yeah. We're eating pizza. And I'm thinking."

"Thinking what?"

He looked up at Callie. "I'm thinking we should leave soon. At least, I should."

She stilled. Her face, open with trust, closed, and her eyes, lit with joy, dimmed. Her lashes lowering, she set her half-eaten slice of pizza on her plate.

A sound distracted him, something pounding down the staircase. He remembered the cat, though it sounded more like a large dog.

"We'll talk later," he said to Rick then turned the phone off.

The cat darted into the kitchen and jumped on Callie's lap, making a mewling sound. A sound of comfort. It felt to him that the cat could read her mood.

"I don't know how anyone isn't claiming her," he said.

She petted the cat, not looking up at him. "Sometimes people have something precious, and they throw it away."

He touched her arm, and she twitched hard. He drew his hand back.

"I have a stalker."

She glanced up, one line furrowed in her forehead.

"It's possible she hurt a woman I'd been...friendly with a few years ago."

"A woman you were sleeping with." She looked at him now, still petting the cat. "What happened? Was she hurt badly?"

"She was pushed down steps at a hotel where the band was staying. She broke a leg. She filed a police report, but no one could prove anything."

Callie's hand stilled on the ebony fur for a few seconds, then she continued petting the cat. "Did she heal well?"

He nodded. "It was a clean break. We still hear from her once in a while. She's training for a marathon."

"I'm glad."

"Yeah, well, we're glad, too."

"You're positive it was the stalker who pushed her?"

"No, but the stalker went on our message board and said things like she deserved what happened to her. A few other creepy things, though she never took credit for it." He frowned. "But there was an incident more recently in Denver. A couple years ago. Another woman said she was pushed down a flight of stairs at a place where we were playing. This time, the stalker claimed she did it."

"Was she hurt?"

"She was drunk, and her worst injury was a chipped tooth."

"Why would your stalker push her down—"

"She said I kissed the other woman."

"Did you?"

"It's possible." He shrugged.

She looked at him, her expression serious. "Does that happen often?"

"Women being pushed down steps? Just the two times, and we're not sure about that."

"The kisses."

"Not often." He picked his words carefully. Her expression was neutral, but he knew he was on rocky waters. "Rick gets that request a lot more than I do. Drummers aren't as sexy."

"It's not the drum, it's the man."

He smiled at her, but she didn't smile back.

"So, you can't be sure it's the stalker."

"Truth is, I'm not sure of much. Music, maybe. And the way I feel about you."

Her face softened, and he felt the softening inside him. It couldn't end here. Somehow he had to fix it.

"We reported it to the police," he said, frowning. "I don't think they believed us. The message came from a cyber café in Phillie, and the police couldn't trace it any farther. The detective told us that if they knew anything, they would call us."

"Don't call us," she said, "we'll call you."

His mood grim, he nodded.

"You think it's her, don't you??"

"There was one more. About a year ago. She didn't take credit for it, but the girl was hurt pretty badly."

"A *girl?*"

"Not a girl but young. Maybe nineteen or so. We were playing at a Dallas club. Lenny and Rick were doing a guitar duel when the girl climbed up on the stage. She held her hand out to me, and we danced." He pictured her pixie face. She'd laughed with her mouth and her eyes. Her hair had been half purple and half blond. At the end of the dance, they'd kissed, and the crowd had roared their approval.

"What happened?" Callie asked.

"A couple days later, a Dallas sax player Rick and I knew got hold of me. He'd been at the club with his wife, and he told us someone pushed the girl into traffic in front of a bus."

Her breath sucked in on a gasp. "He was sure it was the same girl?"

"His wife remembered her hair. The news report said it was right after the show. Whoever did it wore one of those long scarf things over her head, covering her hair and hiding her face. The girl had a broken collar bone from hitting the street. A bus swerved, but it still ran over her hand and crushed bones."

"Oh no." Her horrified expression showed her sympathy.

"Yeah. We called the Dallas police and told them about the stalker, but it was pretty clear they thought we wanted the publicity."

"Did your stalker claim credit for it on your message board?"

"Not this time. The girl was hurt pretty badly. If she were caught, she might get jail time. Maybe she was scared."

"Maybe it wasn't her," she said.

"Maybe," he said slowly. "Since that last time, I've been careful what I do in public. Real careful. I don't want to endanger anyone. Especially you. I can't take the chance that you might be hurt."

Her brow furrowed. "But to change your plans because of the threat... When there's no concrete proof? It seems like an extreme reaction."

"My instincts are shouting at me to get out. I'd rather be extreme than have you hurt." He put his hand on her arm, and he saw sadness in her shadowed eyes. "It doesn't mean we have to separate. But I can't protect you here. Not twenty-four hours of every day."

She blinked. "Twenty-four hours a day? I'm not the president."

"To me, you're more important than the president. Come with us, and I'll make sure you're protected. I'll hire someone to watch you."

"Stay with you while you tour?"

"Yes." He didn't take his gaze from her. He'd pay extra for her room. Sometimes they still slept on the bus to save money. They weren't an A act. Not yet. And touring was expensive. And tiring. And when they weren't on stage, it could get boring.

She smiled at him, but it was a sad smile. "I could visit you sometimes...but a whole tour..." She shook her head. "That's not a good life for me."

"I can't protect you here. I'll have to leave. It's the only way I can make sure the stalker won't come after you."

"I'm going to miss you." Her voice was husky and low, her smile sad.

His jaw clenched, and he fought back a blackness that wanted to descend on him. "I'm not going to let her win. I'll hire an investigator to look into this. I don't care what it costs."

"You should care." She put her palm over his right hand, and her touch was cool.

"Money doesn't matter. *You* matter."

Her fingers curled around his hand. "Do you have to leave now? Can you stay overnight?"

He closed his eyes. Could he? Her breath puffed against his mouth before her lips touched his. The cat mewled and jumped off her, brushing against his leg.

Then he was kissing her, his arms around her, crushing her to him, the blackness rushing away. He wanted to hold her forever, but all he had was this one night, and he vowed to make the best of it.

19

She woke up, and with her eyes still closed, she knew it was still nighttime, and she knew the other side of her bed was empty. Though she lay under her covers, her skin still heated from sleep, a chill started from inside her chest.

Shivering, she opened her eyes to the darkness, knowing instantly that Sam wasn't lying next to her. They'd only been together again for such a short time. So how was it that not hearing his breaths beside her made her feel alone?

Had he left already? Without saying good-bye?

Her hands curled tightly, and she clenched her teeth, telling herself it was a good thing, he didn't want to wake her, he—

A noise downstairs caught her attention. It could've been the cat, but her hands uncurled, and her teeth unclenched, and the small bit of moisture in her eyes dried. She sat straight up from a flat-on-her-back position, as if she'd been doing sit-ups for years, when she hadn't done any since high school. Without pausing, she leapt onto the floor, switched on the light, pulled on her loose capris and a sweatshirt, stuffed her feet into her suede slippers, then hurried downstairs.

Sounds still drifted up to her, and she warned herself not to get too happy. It could be the cat.

But as she neared the bottom of the steps, she heard Sam's voice very clearly. A raspy, tuneful murmur from her kitchen. She also heard something tapping on her counter.

She stopped, leaned against the stairwell, and closed her eyes. *He's here. Still here.* Her body slowly got the message her mind was transmitting, and she relaxed against the banister.

Her heart, which had been pounding hard, slowed. She straightened, held her head high, put on a smile like another woman would put on makeup, then took the last two steps. The tapping continued in the kitchen, and she realized it was in a rhythmic manner. And the murmur... It wasn't a murmur, it was a song.

As she headed into the kitchen, she could hear his words.

"...I fell in love with her voice before I ever saw her face. She isn't the only woman with laughter like a song. She's just the only one for me."

She stopped in the entranceway, and he turned to her, his smile twisted, holding a wooden spoon that he'd been using to tap a tune on the counter.

"Is that about me?" She felt...honored and walked toward him. It felt as if her heart was swelling.

He nodded.

"What's the title?"

His eyes averted from hers, and he angled his head down. "I'll finish this later." He pressed something on a cell phone on the counter.

"You're recording a song on your phone?"

He nodded. "I'm sending it to myself."

She reached him and touched his arm. He was wearing his black jeans and a blue sweatshirt that he'd told her reminded him of her eyes. "If you don't want to tell me the title of your song then don't."

"Okay." He wrapped his arms around her, and whispered in her ear, "Then I won't."

She leaned against him. It was nearly two in the morning. The song title didn't matter. "I should be sleeping."

"Me, too. I have to leave early this morning."

She lifted her head. "I'm going to miss you."

"I'll miss you more."

She stared into his eyes, unable and unwilling to smile and play the game of who would miss whom more. Because she knew she was the winner. He could lose himself in his music, and though she could lose herself in a book, it wouldn't be the same thing. Every romance she started, every kiss on the pages, every love scene she read on her e-reader would remind her of him.

"I don't know what will happen on tour," he said.

She tensed, taking that to mean he wouldn't be celibate. "We haven't made any promises," she said, trying to sound casual, "so we won't break any."

His hold on her tightened then loosened, as if he realized the celibacy issue went both ways. And so it did. She wasn't a nun. He wasn't the only man in the world.

His song had been about a girl who was the only one for him, but they both knew that was a lie.

She drew away from him. He watched her, his eyes dark with emotion. Impossible to read.

So she just had to go with her own needs. She held out her hand. "Come to bed?"

He took it, and they walked to the stairway, passing the cat who was peering up at them. Her attack cat, she thought again, remembering how the cat had protected her from Paul. The thought made her happy.

Then they headed up the staircase, and she stopped thinking about the cat as the need built up in her, higher and faster than before.

This might be her last time with him, and she was going to make it count.

In her bedroom, she turned to him...and he took over, holding her, his lips against hers, and her body blazed up like a newly lit match. Flaming high.

* * *

"The band has a five-year plan," he said in the kitchen in his T-shirt, boxers and socks while she wore a purple robe.

"You worked hard for this." Her voice was soft, and he heard the languid notes of sex in it.

"We're hungry." He was literally hungry. They both were satisfying their after-sex food cravings, standing and eating, leaning against the kitchen counter. He was holding a bowl of chocolate chunk ice cream, and she was nibbling on dark chocolate mint.

"You love it," she said.

He didn't answer right away, sucking on a spoonful of ice cream, swallowing it, feeling it slide down his throat. "Playing in front of people who love our music is a damn great feeling. It's like making love to a hell of a lot of people at once. They're clapping and whistling and shouting." He paused, and she stared at him, not talking, waiting for him to continue. "It's addictive. It gets into your blood."

"Again," she said, "you love it."

"I love making music. Touring can be a drag, but when you're playing in front of the audience, it all changes. The crappy food, the crick in your neck from sleeping on someone's couch that's too soft or too hard... None of it matters. Only the audience."

She didn't say a word, just looked at him, compelling him to explain. He needed her to understand why they did this.

"Touring is like a beast that needs to be fed. And then fed again. Even with the Grammy, we're not making much money yet. Everything we make above living wage, we're socking away for when we make our next album. We're nowhere near famous. We'll still be sleeping in our bus often. When we do get rooms, most of the time we'll still be doubling or tripling up."

"What about the money?"

"This is our first successful album. There are a lot of people who take a chunk: Booking agents, managers, record labels, the other band members, crew, the government..." He shook his head. "In the beginning, it's all about the fame and recognition. Not money. Not yet."

She stared at him, not saying anything, just looking. He normally didn't talk about the dark side of the industry, but he felt compelled to tell her, to make her understand.

"I even feel lucky to have a bus. In the beginning, we just had a van. We're lucky we've built up a following through the years." He frowned, because one of the followers might be a danger to Callie.

"You're good," she said. "Even before this last one."

"You listened to my songs."

"Maybe." She laughed. "So now you have a bigger following."

"Yes, and we're booked in bigger venues, and if we don't fill them, there won't be a next tour." He shrugged. "This was our dream, Rick's and mine, since we first left Eagleton."

"After the graduation party." Her voice was flat.

He nodded. "We never had a Plan B. Justen's the same. It's her dream, too. And Lenny, our bassist, is all for it."

"What about your other band member?"

"You've been following us?" The thought made him feel lighter.

"Maybe." She grinned, but her eyes still remained sad.

He wanted to kiss her but held back. Not yet. "Trish is a temp. She's only been with us a couple months. Our previous keyboardist is taking time off. Family problems. We're hoping he comes back soon."

A slight frown flickered on and off her forehead. "I hope he comes back soon, too. So, you were talking about your plan..."

"If we last five years," he said, "we should be solid enough to take some time off, and not just for recording. Travel for enjoyment. Or just stay home for a few months and watch TV and spend time with the family."

"Until then, you'll feed the beast."

"Gotta do it." He paused and looked at her serious face, and he *needed* to explain what was so important to make him walk away from the best thing that had ever happened to him.

Or maybe he wasn't saying all this to convince her. Maybe he was saying it to convince himself.

"There's magic in music, and for every person who's nodding his head in tune to a beat or moving his body, the magic multiplies. It's like"—he held out his hands—"making love to multitudes of people."

"It's what you want, isn't it?" she asked. "With all your heart."

He took her hands in his. "With half my heart. The other half wants to stay right here."

Her sad smile curved up again, and he ached inside his chest.

"Is that the half below your belt?"

He laughed softer than he normally would. Because everything hurt so much more than usual. Because he felt so much more than usual.

"I want it with all of my body. And all of my heart."

"Perhaps you have two hearts," she said, and the sadness in her voice was like a slow river in danger of drying up, "and they each want something different."

"Maybe there's a way to make it work."

She didn't answer. Instead, she pushed away from the counter and held out her hand. "Come. Let's go upstairs. Can you stay and sleep with me?"

"I plan to do a lot more than sleep."

Her eyebrows rose. "So soon?"

"Not soon. Late. Nine years too late."

He took her hand, and he walked up the steps with her. Pushing down the sadness, because there wasn't much he could do about tomorrow. And he couldn't make up for all the years with her that he'd missed.

All he had right now was right now.

And what he planned to make in the next few hours was five years of memories.

20

"I heard you had some excitement in your life." Sharon, the library director, hopped her short, stubby body onto the high stool behind the reference desk. This move made her a couple of inches taller than Callie. Sharon's maple-brown eyes were as bright as her short, burgundy-colored hair that stood straight up in clumps.

In real time, she was about fifteen years older than Callie. In psychological years—or heart years—she was a rebellious teenager. A brilliant teen, which was why she was the director and Callie's boss.

Callie looked up from the book that, from the yellowed pages, appeared to have been dumped into a toilet. She put it aside and got out one of her homeopathic wipes from the container next to the computer screen. She was pretty sure Sharon was talking about the tussle with Paul outside the bar.

"I gained a cat and lost a boyfriend, if that's what you meant by excitement."

"A kitty?" Sharon's expression softened. "Pictures, please."

A woman at the desk by a window, a regular who was paging through a reference book on flowers, glanced at them, though Sharon's voice only carried when she wanted it to. Or was she looking at Callie, wondering what was different with her?

After the last couple nights, Callie felt as if she glowed with sexual satisfaction, surrounded by a brilliant red aura. She was a changed woman, exposed to the delight of the multiple O.

Wrestling her thoughts into the everyday, she pulled out her cell phone and showed Sharon the four pictures in which the cat didn't blend into the shadows. One was on her pillow, the most comfortable spot in the house.

Looking at the pictures, Callie inhaled deeper and slower. Nothing like pet pictures to lower her blood pressure and bring her mind back to normal.

"A black cat. Very handsome." Sharon glanced up into Callie's eyes. "You got the better end of the trade."

She closed the phone. "You don't like Paul? You never told me."

"I don't like men who act as if they're smarter than me or any other woman."

Callie winced. Yes, that was Paul.

"Especially since I'm much smarter than ninety percent of the men." Sharon didn't smile. It was a fact of life, and Callie nodded. Sharon liked men and had a man friend...or two. Or even more. She was discreet, so Callie wasn't quite sure. All she knew was that Sharon blew the stereotype of the staid librarian out of the building.

Not like her. Callie's cheeks warmed. At least

not until these last few days.

"That wasn't all you traded Paul for," Sharon said. "Unless the gossip is wrong."

Callie moaned quietly, so as not to disturb the library patron by the window. She'd thought she and Sam were discreet, but he had parked in front of her house last night. "I don't know what you heard, but it wasn't a trade."

Sharon's thin eyebrow arched. "Oh?"

"He's going back on tour."

Sharon patted her shoulder, her features compressed in sympathy. "At least you have the cat."

"I hope I have the cat. So far no one's reported losing a young black female cat. She's settled in, and it seems like she's"—she shrugged, because there was no other word for it—"mine."

"Sometimes it's exactly like that." Sharon nodded. "I've found instant lust with a few men, but never instant love. But I've found instant love with a few felines. What have you named her?"

"Mojo." After Sam's band, but the name fit the cat. Ever since Mojo had come into her life, protecting her from Paul, her mojo had changed. She wasn't sure if it was good or bad. It was just...different.

"I like that." She slid off the chair. "Good mojo. You deserve some."

"Everyone does."

Sharon's eyes narrowed, and she shook her

head. "I can think of a few whom I'd like to see with bad mojo. Including your ex. I heard that he slapped you."

Callie winced.

"If he contacts you," Sharon said in a low, lethal voice, "tell him that if he lays a hand on you again, he'll have me to deal with."

Not waiting for a reply, Sharon hopped off the chair and marched away, her soft-soled shoes quiet on the hard tile.

Feeling weepy, Callie turned back to the computer screen. She might be unlucky in love, but she had a Ninja cat and a Ninja friend.

Who needed men? Not her.

That's what her mind told her. But her heart...her stupid heart...ached. It was taking a while to sink in because her body was still satiated from last night. Still in bliss from their time together.

But it was slowly dawning on her that, once again, Sam Krushing was gone.

And, oh God, she'd not only lost her best friend again, this time she'd lost her lover, too.

21

"How many songs have you sung into your recorder since the tour started?" Sitting cross-legged on her and Rick's bed, the bedspread tossed onto the floor, Justen took off the headphones and gazed up at Sam. Her sleek and shiny black hair fell to her left side, inches below her shoulder, as she tilted her head to watch him. Even though she was wearing an oversized Saints sweatshirt and stretchy black pants and socks, she looked like she could've been posing for a fashion 'zine.

A flush came from the bathroom then the sound of running water. It was nearly noon, which meant they'd missed another complimentary breakfast. Just a couple years ago, they would've set an alarm for the breakfast. Now they could afford to miss it, but he still felt a twinge. They were on the cusp of becoming popular—even big. But they could just as easily be the band that fell off the cusp into obscurity. The band that people used to call a one-hit wonder.

Justen was still staring at him, waiting for an answer. He shrugged, lolling in the one chair in the room. Her gaze narrowed, intensifying, as if she were trying to see into his mind. Her "interrogation look," Rick called it.

"A few songs," Sam said.

"Bullshit. Every day in the bus, you've been mumbling a different new song into your recorder."

"Hey, it's better than listening to Trish and Lenny argue over who's the best rocker that died too early."

"Especially when the answer's so obvious." She shrugged her perfectly rounded shoulders. "Janis Joplin. Any day, any song."

He nodded, though he thought it was a toss-up between Joplin and Stevie Ray Vaughn. But some things weren't worth arguing about. In fact, most things weren't worth arguing about. Everyone thought what everyone thought, and nothing was going to change that.

The bathroom door started to open. Raising his voice, Sam said, "You know, you're too pretty for Rick."

She gurgled a laugh. "I know. He's lucky to have me."

"I agree. My girl's a hottie." Rick strode to the bed and jumped on it as Justen grabbed the pillow and held it between them like a shield.

"Not in front of the kid," she said.

Rick laughed and made a shooing motion at Sam, his arm covered with tats. Rick was the drool guy of the group. He'd changed his style in the last year, his brown-black hair slicked at the sides now, longer on the top. He was on the thin side, fit, but not ripped. Traveling as much as they did, none of them had time for intensive workouts. Yet the girls screamed at Rick, especially when he sang. There were even tweets about his new beard, one faction professing love for his beard, another begging him to shave it off.

"You gotta hear Sam's latest," Justen said.

"You sing it." Sam nodded at her. She'd listened to his last song four times. Humming it on the second. Murmuring the words on the third. Singing it softly on the fourth. "You'll do it better."

"True, I will." She grinned. "Listen to this." She pushed away from Rick and slumped against the bunched-up pillows, then her eyes kind of glazed over, not seeing them, but listening to words in her mind. Finally, she sang his song, her voice low and seductive, like warm maple syrup.

"Let's make love on the kitchen floor, let's make love against the front door. Let's fill this house with memories." Her eyes darkened with sadness. *"So when you're gone, everywhere I look, I'll think of you. Everyplace I touch, I'll see your face. Every room, I'll remember you once loved me."*

She sang two more verses, then, still humming, she blinked as if coming out of a trance. The hum stopped, and she inhaled deeply and exhaled in a whoosh. "That's all I remember. I'll have to write the lyrics down. We'll make some changes, but I love it. What do you think?"

"That's sick." Rick narrowed his eyes at Sam. "You've been singing into your recorder like a madman since the tour began. 'Bout time you let us listen."

Sam shrugged. Some days it seemed to him that he was trying to exorcise his emotions with the songs he played into his recorder. Some were just snippets, and some went on and on. He wasn't writing, he was puking out his emotions. He wasn't sure if any were good or if they were crap. He'd only given in to Justen just now because this howl that had been roaring inside him since they'd left Eagleton wasn't going away. As if there was a wind tunnel inside him, and the wind never stopped. He'd hoped that maybe if he told her, it would die down from a shout to a whisper.

"Give me your recorder," Justen said. "I want to hear the rest."

"I don't know...."

Her eyebrows rose. "I'll tickle you."

He raised his eyebrows back at her. "Anytime. Rick, why don't you take another shower? Your woman wants me, and who am I to deny her?"

She slapped her thigh in laughter, and Rick held up his finger in a shooting motion.

"I'm not any man's woman," Justen said, grinning widely. "I'm my own. Now give me the damn recorder or you'll be sorry."

"I'd do it," Rick said. "Remember the last time she said that to me?"

"The ice bath?" Sam shuddered then shrugged. "Oh, hell, why not? Here." He tossed his recorder at her. As it arced in the air, it felt as if he were sending her a big slice of his heart.

But it wasn't his heart. It was just music. It was just words. It was time to release it, let it go.

The hall door opened, and he forced his gaze from the recorder to Lenny and Trish as they came into the room, Trish in full makeup, though it was just the five of them. She and Lenny sat on the bed, though not close to each other. No magic between them—just occasional and unemotional sex. That was a good thing, since Sam was hoping Frank would come back. Though Trish could play anything they threw at her, the music was always...competent. Okay. Not Frank. Frank made the music sound like magic.

For the next couple hours and a few minutes more, they ate room-service pizza and listened to his recorded songs, his voice sounding like Leonard Cohen on a bad day. The others talked excitedly around him, their words interrupting his thoughts, their voices raised then periods of quiet, interspersed with comments and laughter and humming. And at one point, they talked about another platinum, and maybe a diamond album.

He didn't say anything, because they were listening to his songs in three ways: music lovers, artists and, lastly, as products.

And the truth was that, for him, these were songs carved out of his heart.

Finally the songs stopped, and the last two lines

from his first song hung in the air: *Just remember I love you. No matter what happens, remember that is true. No matter where I am. No matter what I do.*

And as he heard it, Trish got off the bed, took his hand and squeezed it. He squeezed her hand back. She bent down to him. Her blond hair with brown roots brushed her shoulders, paler than Callie's golden-blond hair. Her blue eyes were paler than Callie's, too, and so was her smile. Callie smiled like a kid, with her heart and her eyes as well as her mouth. Trish smiled like she was afraid the world might reject her.

"You miss her."

He nodded.

She squeezed his hand again and released it, sitting back on the bed with Lenny. When she'd first joined their group, Sam would catch her staring at him, and it had made him feel like the neck of his T-shift was too tight. She didn't have Justen's beauty, but not many women did, and there was nothing wrong with her square-shaped face and thin lips. He'd just thought it was better not to get involved with someone he worked with. Someone he knew he would never love. So he'd treated her as a friend, nothing more. He didn't need complications.

"Ya know which is my favorite?" Lenny asked then didn't wait for an answer. "The one about not living life in a straight line."

"If that song isn't about us," Rick said, "I don't

know what is. What else?"

Sam sat up. Only two of his songs had gotten onto the last album. They'd gotten the Grammy for the librarian song, but that was a fluke. He was more of a musician and sometime lyricist than a songwriter. Getting the Grammy had made him feel like the ugly guy who'd gotten lucky with the class beauty.

Justen picked the first song she'd heard, which she'd replayed for them. Trish picked "Just Remember I Love You." She looked down at her lap, and Sam had the idea she was fighting tears. "It's the kind of simple yet heart-warming song that people want. Even when the one you love doesn't love you anymore. Even when it feels like someone's taken an axe to your heart and shredded it, you still want to believe it can happen."

"That's the fairy-tale syndrome." Justen made a face. "The truth is, even Prince Charming has a bit of the frog in him, and maybe Snow White has some, too. But when we find out our guy has warts, we feel betrayed."

"And sometimes we are betrayed," Trish said, her voice turning hard. "A fucking stab in our hearts."

There was silence in the room. Sam broke it. "You're only putting my songs on the album? What about the ones you were working on?" He looked at Rick and Justen.

"Maybe the next one," Rick said.

Justen nodded. "Yours kind of go together. And I really want to sing some of them."

"This will go over big with the brokenhearted crowd." Trish tried to smile, and it failed.

"Hey, that's what we should name it," Lenny said. "*Songs for the Broken-hearted.*"

"Real cheery," Sam said. "No one's gonna want to listen to that."

Rick narrowed his eyes at him. "With these songs, they will. Believe in yourself, dude."

"May as well make some use of your broken heart." Lenny shrugged. "Next year when we're raking in all the Grammys, you'll think that broken heart is the best thing that happened to you. You'll be thanking the chick for turning you down."

"She didn't turn me down. It was my choice. I knew it wouldn't work for either of us." A sudden hurt pierced Sam's chest. There'd been no threats from his stalker for the last two months. He wondered now if he'd been wrong to leave so abruptly.

"Sometimes it feels like we don't have a choice." Trish looked away. "This life we live, it's just not a good fit with marriage." A breathy hitch came from her, close to a sob.

Sam got off his chair then sat on the bed next to her. He tugged her to his side to comfort her, and she clung to him. On her other side, Lenny patted her back.

After a moment, she pulled away. "Sorry."

"You want to talk about it?" Sam asked.

She shook her head. "Nothing to talk about. I've make bad choices, but I'll get over it. I don't want to cry on everyone's shoulders."

"That's what shoulders are for." Justen reached across the divide between the two beds and patted Trish's knee.

Trish gave a laugh that had tears in it. "Let's change the subject." She glanced sideways at Sam. "I gotta tell you, one song of yours bugged me. The one about banging her on the floor and against the door. Do you know how uncomfortable it is being banged against the door?"

"Hey, they show it in movies all the time," Rick said. "Someone must like it."

"The person who wrote the scenes, stupid." Justen poked him in his ribs. "And guess what gender that is?"

Lenny groaned. "Not female. We get the idea."

"It's not our fault we don't know," Sam said. "No one's told us. Write a song about it. Tell the world. Call it, 'Don't Bang Me Against a Door Unless You Want A Pointy Cowboy Boot In Your Happy Place.'"

Rick and Lenny laughed, but the two women stared at him and then slowly looked at each other.

"We totally have to do this," Justen said.

Trish sat up straight. "It's a brilliant idea. I can think of dozens of things to write about."

"What're you talking about?" Rick's sat

straighter and stiffer, his nostrils flared as if he smelled trouble. "We already agreed we're recording Sam's songs."

"Don't worry." The narrow-eyed, black look Justen gave Rick made a lie of her words. "It won't be a band thing. Trish and I will do it on our own dime and with our own musicians."

"I'll be your drummer." Sam patted Trish's back, and she gave him a wobbly smile.

Both Lenny and Rick spoke up, saying they'd play on it.

"And you two broken-hearted geniuses don't need to worry about being alone," Lenny said. "I'll buy Sam a rubber life-sized doll and buy Trish here a vibrator."

Justen and Rick cracked up. Trish raised her eyebrows at Sam. "A rubber doll? Seriously?"

"I'll pass." He reached behind Trish and jabbed Lenny in his shoulder.

Lenny stopped cackling to grab his upper arm. "Anatomically correct, dude. You don't know what you've been missing."

"You're an asshole."

"I'm not hearing any complaints about the vibrator." Lenny raised his eyebrows at Trish.

"Hmmm. Sometimes a vibrator is better than a man."

"I'll second that," Justen said. "We know the best places to use it. Hitting spots men don't always find."

Rick put his hands over his ears. "I don't want to hear this."

She grinned. "And then we can put it away in its drawer."

"And drop off to sleep," Trish said, "and it won't take up three-fourths of the bed. It won't snore and fart and mumble another woman's name. It won't leave a wet spot for you to sleep on. It does its job, and you turn it off, and you're done until the next time you need it."

"I gotta write this down." Justen leaned sideways to the nightstand between the two beds and grabbed a pen and notepad. "That's gotta be on the album."

"An Ode To a Vibrator?" Sam laughed but thought of Callie again. His thoughts always seemed to go back to Callie.

Was she using a vibrator without him?

Or was she using another man?

The last thought made him clench his hands into fists.

Trish touched his shoulder. "That's just sometimes. Other times...I swear, there's nothing like having a warm body next to me. Arms to hold me. Knowing I'm not alone and someone wants me."

He took her hand, squeezed it.

She leaned forward and kissed him, tentative but not sisterly. Nothing sisterly about it.

He pulled away, and her face morphed into

hurt.

"I'll put that into the song, too," Justen said. "Start out angry, then put in the other bit about the warm body, having someone to care."

"Until he doesn't care anymore." Trish turned away from him, her laugh hard.

The atmosphere changed, a dead silence, and he glanced up to see Justen frowning, her gaze twitching to him and Trish while Rick watched them with a half smile. Sam didn't have to look at Lenny to know he was staring at them with speculation, too.

"Men are assholes." Justen slid off her bed. "Let's go to your room. We can record some ideas on your computer."

"Let me know when it's ready." Lenny jerked his finger at his chest. "I'll be your guy."

Trish shook her head, her lips twisted. "I don't think so. I'm going down to the bar."

"A bit early for that."

"I don't give a damn how early it is. Maybe I'll meet a guy. I don't need a vibrator tonight, I need a real man."

There was silence as she strode out, her back stiff. The door closed behind her, and the others looked at Sam, and he shrugged.

Sometimes it seemed like everyone had a bruised heart, and they all handled it different ways.

"Looks like you're not getting lucky anymore."

Rick grinned at Lenny.

"Hey, I'm not the only one." He jerked his chin toward Sam. "Mr. Picky's not getting anything, either."

Sam shrugged. If they only knew, just to have had the short time with Callie made him a lucky man.

Even though he was alone now, he still had his memories.

He closed his eyes. But they weren't enough. He wanted more.

22

Mojo greeted Callie, winding around her ankles, purring. Callie bent, put her hands on Mojo's sides, and kissed her head, like she used to do with Magic. Unlike most cats she knew, Mojo didn't squirm out of her hold.

"I swear, you're a cat-dog combo."

Mojo meowed, and it sounded to Callie as if she was saying yes.

The air conditioner kicked in, sending cooling air into the house. A nice change from the humidity outside that made her hair corkscrew and her skin sweat. She slid off her sandals then lifted Mojo to her shoulder. As she stepped into the kitchen, the cat purred.

"Who needs a man when she has a cat?" Callie asked.

The answer lit up in her mind: *I do.*

She frowned. It had been five months and a bit since the cold, snowy day Sam was in her house, in her bed...and in her.

Time to move on. Past time. She needed to treat what had happened between them like it was a book she loved—because sometimes she loved books more than...well, people. She should X it out on her *Already Read* Excel sheet then go on to the next book on her *To Read* list. One with new pages filled with prose and possibilities.

She sighed, turned her head to kiss the crown of Mojo's head again, then set her on the floor. Her land phone on the counter was blinking with a message. Probably a marketer. She only kept it because all her calls in North America were free with her TV and computer bundle. But some people called her on it, so she stepped over to it and saw there were two messages. She punched it and reached down to unbutton her skirt as the first message started.

Sam's voice came out of it, deep and rich. Her fingers on the button stilled, and she froze, like a child playing the *statue* game.

"The band's going to be in Chicago on Saturday. I haven't heard anything from the stalker since I left Eagleton. Maybe she's attached to someone else now. My parents are driving down and staying overnight. I hope you'll come."

The next phone message started as she unfroze. Her fingers slipping away from her skirt, she recognized Brenda Krushing's husky voice, asking her to drive to Chicago with her and her husband on Saturday and drive back on Sunday. Brenda left her number, though Callie could easily look it up. At one point, when she was about five or six years old, she'd memorized it, but she'd forgotten it by now.

She called Brenda instead of Sam. She wasn't ready to talk to him. Too many butterflies in her stomach, and her throat was tightening, as if she were a teenager. A woman's voice answered the phone, a higher pitched voice than Brenda's. In the background, Callie heard music and realized she'd called during the hour that was probably busy, with people stopping off after work for a drink and some of the sweet potato fries the bar was known for.

The woman put her on hold. In a few seconds, Brenda came on, and they made arrangements, not wasting words. Before she hung up, Brenda asked her not to mention it to anyone. "Just in case the crazy woman is still following the band. You never know. That stuff gets all the social media sites faster than you can blink, and I wouldn't want you to be hurt."

"Neither would I," she said. They hung up, and her heart was beating fast. Of course, she would have to tell her mom and dad, but they would be discreet. They would wish her well, with her mom's eyes anxious, wanting her to be normal. Which, in her eyes, meant married with children. To have the same joy in her husband and child that she had.

What hurt Callie was that she wanted the same thing. And lately, she wasn't sure if it was ever going to happen.

But now she felt as if her heart was typing out a message to her. It said, *Maybe this time.*

She laughed shakily and headed to her bedroom. She always had been a sucker for a love story.

* * *

"She's coming," Brenda said, her voice crackling on the cell phone, the connection not the best.

On the bus, Sam leaned back. "I made reservations for two rooms."

"Rooms?"

"Yes. One under your name, one under Dad's."

Seconds passed, maybe a full minute, before his mom talked. "Okay, your dad and I are paying for ours." Her voice was stronger now, no crackles.

"No, you're not. I already paid for them."

"Sam."

"Mom."

He could feel the eyes of the other bus members on him. Except Rick, whose mom had a bad cold and was going to miss the concert. His dad lived in Oklahoma with his second wife and Rick's half sister, who Rick had never met. It wasn't something he liked to talk about.

"Are you calling her?" Brenda asked.

He breathed in, not answering right away. He didn't know why Callie hadn't called him, but it felt right to do it this way. There were times to race through barriers, and there were times to sit back. This felt like a time to sit back. He'd see her soon, and when he did, he wouldn't tiptoe anywhere.

Maybe she felt the same way.

"No," he said.

Brenda huffed. "You're as stubborn as your dad."

"I think I got that from you."

"See you in Chicago." She laughed and hung up.

He put away his phone and looked out the window. He wasn't sure where they were traveling through, but there were cornfields on one side, and on the other side, there were cows. Indiana maybe? Ohio?

He closed his eyes and pictured Callie. Laughing, pensive, hurt... with her eyes closed and then her mouth open as she moaned with ecstasy.

His hands clenched on his thighs. Soon he would see her. Soon.

"You're expecting family in Chicago?" Trish asked.

"Uh huh." He kept his eyes closed.

"That will be nice."

"Uh huh."

"You're a real conversationalist."

Laughter came from Lenny. "Talk to him about drums and music. Then he'll have something to say."

He kept his eyes closed tight, and he smiled, thinking of Callie. Callie, Callie, Callie. Her name was a song inside him. He would see her soon. And though he trusted his band members, sometimes the best thing to say was nothing.

23

The crowd screamed. The band was hot, and Sam was on fire.

He played like tonight was the only night it mattered.

He played like God and the devil were watching him, and God had first pick, so he damned well better be good or else sharp-toothed minions would be chomping on his heels.

The last time they'd played a Chicago theater, they were the opening act. Now they were the main one. The stars. Though none of them felt like stars. Maybe shooting stars, on their way up, and they hoped they wouldn't plummet soon.

They played for more than three hours and only stopped because of the crew. As always, Sam was completely alive on stage. But tonight, knowing that Callie was in the audience, he was super buzzed. And though he was at the back of the band, playing his drums, he wasn't doing it for the audience.

Tonight was for her. *Callie, Callie, Callie.* Her name ran through his mind with every drumbeat, every heartbeat, every breath.

They played three encores, and then it was done. The standing ovation—or as Justen called it, "the best O ever"—lasted so long that they finally reluctantly left, high from the applause and the perfect storm of music. For the first time in his life, Sam felt like a rock star instead of an overgrown kid who liked to bang on drums because he wasn't good at anything else.

Callie, I hope you know this was for you.

The buzz was still sizzling inside them in their back room with the food, drinks, an olive-green couch that looked like it came from a seventies basement, and some folding chairs. But this was more than they usually had. Like Rick said to Justen when they'd walked in, "This is the high life, baby."

Rick grabbed the bourbon and poured a shot for Sam. Justen did a sexy little dance and said, "We were stars tonight! We were amazing!"

Sam stretched his mouth in a giant smile, and despite his worries, it felt to him that today was *the day*. He wasn't sure what *the day* was. It was just *the day*. The day when he felt the same high as he had at the Grammy show, as if he were at the top of the world....

Except this was better than the Grammys. Callie was here.

They weren't alone much longer. The theater manager popped into the room with a huge grin, happy they'd filled the place and hadn't turned out to be duds. A couple blues singers who'd been around Chicago since before Sam's parents were born came in. Sam and the band members genuflected to them, with show-off Rick going down on both knees and bowing until his forehead touched the floor.

Some guy from a Chicago magazine snapped pictures of them, and Sam would've put down money they were hoping for a shot of Justen's boobs in her low-cut top. It was a fact of life that cleavage sold. The more flesh, the more the coverage, and the hell with talent.

Fake was the new reality, he thought, as he smiled for the bone-thin photographer snapping pictures of him.

The door opened again. It had opened a dozen times already, but suddenly every cell in his body came to attention. He glanced at the door, and there she stood. Callie. Her eyes wide open and staring at him.

He stared back at her, feeling the same way. His whole body happy. A song pounding in his head sang, *Callie's here. You can be happy now. This is what it's all about.*

"That's it!" the photographer called out. "That's the rock star money shot. I'll call it 'The drummer with the world at his feet.'"

And that's when Sam thought, *oh fuck*, and he almost turned away from Callie and his parents.

He should've told them not to come to the back room, just in case the stalker was after him, but it was too late now. The photographer had a hungry look on his face. If Sam took him aside and asked him not to take a picture of Callie, explaining that a stalker had threatened any woman he went out with, before he finished the sentence, the photographer would be snapping pictures of Callie like they were golden. Not caring if she was hurt or killed. Only caring about the money it would bring him.

"My family's here," he muttered then headed over to them. He hugged Callie, his mom and dad. He thought of whispering in Callie's ear that she should pretend to be his sister. But he peered behind him, and the photographer was snapping pictures of Rick and Justen, locked together in a kiss. The real money shot.

Relief slammed through him.

Trish walked over to them, shaking hands and telling his mom and dad that he was a genius. His mom grinned and said she always knew it. His dad, who left most of the talking to his mom, just grinned.

And Callie...she didn't grin, a small frown on her forehead. Probably the same way he looked when he walked into a library and thought, *What the hell am I doing here?*

Looking at her, the only woman he'd loved besides his mother, he felt an empty, aching hole inside his chest, and he knew the hole would fill up only if she stayed.

He couldn't fuck this up. He couldn't.

"Are you okay?" Trish curved her hand on his

arm.

He peered down, and it felt as if he were looking at her in a drunken dream, seeing her worried forehead and the puckering skin around her eyes.

"Don't worry," she said. "I'll take care of everything."

Her words echoed in his mind, and he shook his head.

"That's okay." Callie stepped to his side and put her arm around him. "I'll take care of him."

He looked away from Trish to Callie, who tugged him away from Trish. He stumbled, falling against her, making her stagger, and he was sorry for it. Then she was holding him, and he wasn't sorry for that, though he could tell other people were looking at him, laughing at them.

He remembered thinking that Justen had Rick on a leash. Him, too. But not with Justen. With Callie.

He liked his leash. "I'm your dog."

"Your what?"

"Your dog. Don't sha know?" He was slurring his words. He'd only had the one drink and no drugs. "You're intoxicatin' me."

Her laugh was shaky as she steered him to the chairs against the wall. "You're dehydrated. You're not thinking right. It's making you lightheaded." She looked at one of the older blues guys who was getting up from a chair. "Thanks so much."

"No problem," he said. "I've been intoxicated by

a beautiful lady before, too."

Everyone around her laughed, and she smiled at him then turned her attention to Sam as she lowered him to the chair, where he immediately pulled her onto his lap.

Laughter started again, and her cheeks reddened.

In his mind, he knew he should be thinking of the stalker, but it didn't seem to matter. Nothing mattered.

"You need water," she said.

"Need you."

Her expression changed to sadness. He closed his eyes. It hurt him to witness her unhappiness. He wanted to do something about it, wanted to make her smile and laugh, but he was too weak. He wanted to be strong for Callie instead of dizzy.

"Love you, Callie. Always loved you."

A sound that could've been a laugh or a cry came from her. His eyes closed, and he tried to push back the dizziness. Something was wrong with him. Callie was here, and this was what he wanted more than anything. But he was sick, and that would ruin everything. What was wrong with him to get sick now?

"Here's water." Trish's voice. He opened his eyes.

"Thanks." Callie took a clear plastic water bottle from Trish and gave it to him. "Drink this."

He wrapped his hand around the cool plastic then jerked it up. Water sloshed on him, and he realized the bottle top was off. He put it to his mouth because he didn't want to be sick. He wanted to be healthy and happy.

She started to pull off his lap, and he put his arm around her waist, holding her back.

Because, most of all, he wanted to be with Callie.

24

Callie was watching him closely. Once he'd drunk a bottle and a half of water and eaten some cookies, he was better and embarrassed, apologizing to everyone. But he was talking to a crowd that apparently had seen a lot worse—and done a lot worse. The two old blues guys proceeded to tell the room about it, naming famous names.

That's when he'd taken her hand and snuck out of there with everyone's attention on the blues guys.

The hotel was only two blocks away from the theater. They took the elevator to the fourth floor. They were the only ones on it, but the walls were glass, and he whispered to her that he didn't want to kiss her where anyone could see them.

Maybe that was a good thing, she thought, as they both breathed in gulps and watched the floor numbers light up.

She could have insisted they talk. That she hated this on-again-off-again thing. But she would be lying if she said she didn't want this. And if they talked and he gave the wrong answers, and she had to walk away from him—for good this time— she would never forgive herself for not doing this first.

The elevator door opened, and he stood back to

let her exit first. As she stepped out, she felt as though her whole body was wide open, like a cartoon with her heart popping in and out and beating like one of his drums.

They stopped in front of his door, and he used the key card to open it. Then they were inside, and he pushed her against the door and kissed her. Not saying a word. Just kissing her as if he were desperate. She twisted her leg around his thigh and grabbed on to him, and wanted to do it right there. Right this second.

He pulled away, breathing heavily.

"Why did you stop?" she asked.

"Have you ever had sex against the door?"

She shook her head. She'd had sex in a car, in a bed, and once outside on a blanket on the grass.

"Someone told me it's not fun for the ladies."

A laugh shook her, and she recalled that having sex outside on the blanket hadn't been fun, either. The ground beneath the thin blanket had been hard and bumpy. When it was over, her boyfriend had flopped onto the blanket next to her and said, "That was awesome."

She'd turned her head to look at his smug expression, so pleased with himself and not asking how she felt. She wasn't a hater, but for that second, she'd hated him.

"What are you thinking?" he asked.

"I think we should get to the bed as soon as possible."

He grinned. "I'll beat you."

Laughing, she ran, but he bounded past her.

They tumbled into bed and undressed each other, then she rolled off the bed to use the bathroom. Looking at herself in the mirror, she bemoaned her lack of toothpaste, but she breathed on her cupped hand and her breath smelled just fine. Besides, he'd kissed her before and hadn't complained.

She puffed up her hair then asked herself why she was so nervous. They'd done this before. Done it very well, too.

Thinking about it, she moaned then put her hand over her mouth.

The bathroom door opened. And there he stood, her beautiful man with his beautiful body and his proud penis swollen up nicely with blood and desire.

"Are you getting cold feet?" he asked.

"My feet might be cold." She stepped toward him. "But the rest of me is pretty damn hot."

He made a sound, and she wasn't sure if it was a cry or a laugh. He drew her against him, and they kissed with his erection snuggled against her belly.

But that wasn't the place where she wanted it to snuggle.

She pushed away from him, and before she could say anything, he bent and slid an arm behind her knees and the other behind her back, and he swept her up while she yelped and hung on to him.

"I won't drop you," he said.

Not tonight, she thought. But what about tomorrow?

She wiped that thought from her mind. Not tonight. Tonight she wasn't going to think, she was going to act. Even better, she was going to *love*.

He swept the bedspread to the floor then laid her onto the bed and kissed her from her head to her toes while she clutched the pillow beneath her head. Until tonight, she hadn't realized that her toes were erogenous zones. She moaned and made squeaky noises and mewling noises, and finally she begged him to hurry up and make love to her.

She watched him while he put on a condom, the seconds stretching out. Then he was between her legs and inside her as she clasped his shoulders, her feet braced on the bed, her knees up. They moved in a fast and hard lover's dance, just what she wanted. She'd been waiting for this. Waiting too long.

She slapped her hands against the headboard to keep her head from pounding into it. And it was so great, so great, so fanfreakingtastic great. And finally—finally—he collapsed on top of her, and she held him tightly, never wanting to let him go.

They remained like that for moments until his racing heartbeat slowed and he exhaled slow and long, and she smiled because it was the sound of a man who had been fully spent in one of the most primitive sources of satisfaction.

And she felt slightly sore inside from their vigorous coupling but fully pleasured. Her body saying, *That was amazing.*

It was saying something else, too.

"I'm hungry," she said.

"I'm hungrier," he said.

"We need to get up," she said, still not moving, her body too languid and happy to roll out of bed.

"I know." He rolled off her then lay unmoving by her side.

She slowly turned her head to him. "Did you know you're the greatest lover on earth?"

"I always suspected." He turned his head to grin at her.

"It's true. You are."

"I'll have to write a song about it."

She laughed and finally rolled out of bed then headed to the bathroom to wash up.

Less than ten minutes later, they headed to the elevator, and they both became quiet, their smiles gone. She didn't know why he was so quiet, but she was thinking about the talk they needed to have.

* * *

At an all-night diner two blocks from the hotel, Sam stuffed himself with food. Without Callie, his appetite had been shut off. He'd eaten because he'd needed food to live, but everything had tasted bland, everything had felt dull, everything but the music.

But now, the grilled chicken sandwich with jack cheese and avocado tasted like ambrosia. Who knew the small diner, with small round tables and wicker chairs, one of the few places open at four a.m., would serve food like this? The sweet potato fries on the side reminded him of the sweet potato fries his parents made for the bar patrons, though the diner's cook didn't spice them up with cayenne pepper like his mom did.

Callie was eating off the appetizer menu. He ate two of her four small crab cakes that she said were two too many, and she swiped sweet potato fries from his plate.

That's what couples did. For the first time since he was an adult—since he was six—he was a part of a couple. One out of two.

There was so much happiness in him. And he knew that deep down inside him, he was still the little kid working hard to impress a girl at recess.

They ate in silence, and it wasn't uncomfortable. He was too stuffed with fulfillment, and he just thought about the food and the music and, most of all, Callie. Her sitting next to him, eating hungrily, making *hmmm* sounds as she ate, her eyelids closed, as if in bliss. Just as she'd done while they made love.

Another image of her face during their lovemaking snapped into his mind: her face intensely alive and filled with tension, with power, with the joy of the moment, making the meeting of their eyes as well as the meeting of their bodies part of the joy, the soaring ecstasy, and then the completion.

Which reminded him...

"Dessert?" he asked.

She pushed her empty plate away. "I don't know if I can eat another bite. But I did see bread pudding on the menu. My grandmother used to make it. We could split it." She groaned. "I might not fit back into my clothes."

"We'll have to do another round of exercise. You can go on top. Ride me like I'm a wild stallion. I won't mind." He grinned. "And if you don't fit back into your clothes, I won't mind that, either."

She laughed. "You're a devil. I'll be lucky if I can walk out of here, much less ride anything or anyone. You might have to carry me out."

The waitress, a small woman who wore too much makeup and had hair an impossible bright red color, came for their dessert choice and to take away their dishes. Glancing at Callie's face, Sam saw a line furrowing her forehead, as if the small action stripped away some of the carefree happiness.

Her gaze met his, the light in her eyes dimmed. A small ache burrowed into his chest. Things had to be said, decisions needed to be made. He wished he could put it off longer, but she would be leaving for home in a few hours.

"We have to talk," she said.

He put his hand on hers. "Not now. Let's wait until after we eat dessert."

She nodded and managed a smile.

They talked about small stuff while they waited for the pudding. The cat, his dad and mom, her parents. And more emotions filled him. Good ones. There was no talk about his career or music—that would come later. But right now, she was a piece of home. They didn't have to be funny or flirty or phony, like his conversations with other women often seemed to be, as if they were performing for invisible cameras. Making him step back and long for his drums.

He didn't long for his drums now. He reached across the table to hold her hand resting on it. Her words trailed off, and they just smiled and gazed at each other, and that was...almost enough.

25

The waitress came with the bread pudding. Callie ate a bite, her eyes closed to focus on the taste. Like the rest of the meal, it was wonderful, reminding her of Sunday dinners at her grandmother's. Something else to remember, along with all the other memories she was storing in her mind.

Opening her eyes, she looked straight at Sam and smiled at him.

"What?" he asked.

"I was thinking that the pudding was a piece of home in Chicago. And then I looked at you, and I thought you're my piece of home." In Chicago, she added silently. And wherever else she might be with him.

"I was thinking the same thing about you." He paused, his eyes darkened. "What about Nashville? Would that be a home to you if I were there?"

She sat back, and the muscles of his face tightened. With a silent sigh, she leaned toward him again.

She didn't know what she wanted.

No, that wasn't true. She wanted him. But not just for one night.

"What about your tour?"

"We're cutting the tour short."

"You can do that?"

"There's no shortage of bands and singers. They'll find someone to fill it. Like we did tonight." His lips screwed downward. "Music has more talent than any other business I can think of. You've got someone big and immovable ahead of you. And you've got a multitude of someones behind you who want to be even bigger."

"And you wouldn't do anything else," she said. "It's not a very secure occupation. Don't you ever worry?"

He didn't answer right away, seriously thinking about her question. "I can always get a job playing drums. I *want* more than just a job, and I'll do everything I can to make it work. But if the band flops and goes away, I'll still be okay, doing what I want and what makes me feel good."

She put her hand over his. And he put his over hers. As if they were making a wordless pact.

"I won't get as much money, but as long as I'm healthy, I'll be able to support my family in a decent style."

He was giving her a message. She nodded. She had her degree. She made a modest living. If they lived fairly frugally, she could support him...and their children.

Her heart beat faster. It wasn't *things* that she needed.

"The band planned to put together an album early next year," he continued, "but we have enough songs for a new album already, so we decided not to wait. We're renting a house in Nashville with a studio for three months. Would you stay with me?"

She stared at him and swallowed. "We? You're all staying together at the house?"

"It has three bedrooms and a guesthouse. I already told them I'll pay extra for the guesthouse. It's in a gated community, otherwise I wouldn't have gone."

"I thought you weren't worried about the stalker anymore."

"I'm not worried, but I'm careful. Especially if you're going to stay with us."

"Will any of the others have guests? Will I be the only non-musician?"

"Yes, but we won't be isolated. You won't have to stay locked up. Nashville is a great city. Friendly. I think you'll enjoy it. I could introduce you to other people."

"Other musician wives and girlfriends?"

He nodded.

She turned her head away. She'd be the "girlfriend." How odd. She was used to being the center of her own life. If she said yes, she'd be on the periphery of his.

"I didn't realize before now how much I was asking of you," he said. "I was just thinking we'd be together."

She clasped her hands in her lap.

"You'd have to leave your job." His tone flattened. "You'd be away from your mom and dad and friends. And I can't even tell you how much we'll be together, because sometimes making the record is an all-day thing going into the night. And when I'm in the middle of my music, I'm a selfish bastard."

Gazing at the remains of her bread pudding, she bit down on her lower lip.

"I was just thinking that I'd be in one place," he continued, "and it would be like a honeymoon. That it would be a chance to see if it would work out. But I was lying to myself. I see now that it wouldn't be. Of course you don't want to go."

Slowly, she raised her head. Before she could say anything, he leaned toward her. "Would you spend a few weekends with me?"

She took a deep breath. "A few weekends wouldn't be enough for me. I'd need a longer time than that."

His eyes brightened. "Any time you can stay will be a good time. I will love you every night."

She laughed and heard a sob in it. "I won't make you promise that, though it would be lovely."

"Good. Because sometimes I'll love you during the day."

"Even if I come for the full three months?"

He stilled, but his eyes...they blazed.

"I might not have to quit my job. I have vacation time coming." Three weeks this year. She usually took off Christmas week and didn't come back until the New Year. She'd been thinking of flying to London to visit a librarian friend there. "I could ask for a leave of absence."

"You would do that? What about your parents? Your mom is okay now?"

She closed her eyes. That was the tough part. She took a deep breath, opened her eyes. "She's doing...all right now. She's participating in a clinical trial, and her health seems to be improving. But she already told me that even if her condition gets worse, she doesn't want me to stay because of her. She wants me to live my life to the fullest."

"Your mom's an amazing woman."

"I know. And she has my dad, too, and my aunt and other relatives."

"And you'd be a short plane trip away."

The waitress was coming their way. Callie swallowed and looked at him. "Let's go back to the hotel."

As the waitress reached their table, he told her they were ready for their check. She asked if they wanted the pudding boxed, and Sam said no, and at the same time, Callie said yes.

Sam looked at her then back to the waitress. "Whatever the lady wants, the lady gets."

She laughed and heard the catch in her voice again. As the waitress left with the pudding and the plates and silverware, Sam leaned forward and gave her a hard kiss. "I mean that. I can't give you the moon. Not yet. But one day I might. And when I do—"

"Stop." She put her fingers over his lips. "I don't want the moon. I just want you."

His eyes darkened. He reached up to hold her hand, and he kissed her fingers then her palm. "I'm the luckiest man in the world."

"Yes, you are."

"As well as the best lover."

She laughed again, this time with no catch. No uncertainties. "I loved you when I was four years old. It's crazy to say that I would never love anyone else, but I never have. And I tried. I tried hard. I'm young yet, I know, but I can't imagine loving another man the way I love you. I don't think it's possible. When you came back into my life, I thought you might be a fling. But the only thing that's flung is my heart. Right into your hands."

"Callie..." His voice broke, and he stared into her eyes. He shook his head, swallowing, his Adam's apple bobbing.

The waitress came with the container of pudding and the bill, leaving them on the table. Sam waited for her to leave before speaking.

"I have one word for everything you said to me."

"One word?" She smiled at him. She didn't know what was going to happen to him or to her...but she was happy. Right in this moment, she was deliriously, deliciously happy.

"Ditto."

She laughed, and then she leaned over to kiss him. A long, hard kiss, branding him as hers. He drew away from her first. When they stood, she saw there were only a few couples at the other tables but everyone smiled indulgently at them, their happiness making the others happy for the instant, she thought, the way watching the cat sleep gave her the *awww* feeling, temporarily warming that cold, empty ache in her chest that came from missing Sam.

They headed to the door, her with her purse and him with the boxed pudding. "How are we going to eat this?" he asked.

"Our fingers?"

He gave her a sideways glance, his mouth crooked up and the skin around his eyes crinkling. "I could smear it over your body then lick it off."

"Or I could smear it over yours."

"I have a long body. It wouldn't cover much."

Two older men came into the place, and they stepped back to let the two pass. As she waited, she turned to him.

"It would cover the important part."

He smiled slowly. His hand clasped her arm, and he pulled her to him, holding her against him, tight. His mouth came down on hers, and it felt to her like the honeymoon that wasn't really a honeymoon had started already.

And she knew why she was really doing this.

Because if she didn't, for the rest of her life, she

would always wonder if she'd thrown out the best thing in her life. So she clung to him, because she didn't know for sure what would happen later.

She only knew what was going to happen now.

26

Sam met the band members for a late breakfast. The others came in pairs. Justen and Rick were a given, but he raised his eyebrow at Lenny and Trish walking into the open dining area, Trish's hand looped possessively through Lenny's elbow.

Good. She'd shifted her interest to Lenny again. Trish had to know by now that faithfulness wasn't his strongest character trait, and it would be a temporary hookup. But maybe that's all she wanted, too. Nothing wrong with temporary.

They gathered around a round table in the dining area, laughing and talking about last night. They'd already gotten a rave review in the *Chicago Tribune*.

"Awesome night," Sam said. "We killed it."

"I don't think that's all you killed." Lenny snickered.

"Real classy." Justen gave him her witch's eye.

"Hey, just sayin' what the rest of you are thinkin'."

Sam took a bite of his eggs and thought about last night's after-sex dinner. He missed Callie already. When he'd walked her to the lobby this morning, she'd sported a pink stubble rash on her chin. His mom had shaken her head but had done a lousy job of holding back a smile, just as she'd done at school when his second grade teacher had complained that he'd tapped his Number 2 pencils on the desk like they were drums, and she'd recognized the Rolling Stones song, "Sympathy For The Devil."

It felt odd now to be just the five of them and no Callie. Her memory was more real and vital than the bodies at the table.

"Don't make a big deal out of it," he said. "The only thing I know right now is that I'm hungry."

"You're not worried about the stalker?" Lenny asked.

"Not today, I'm not."

Rick looked at Justen. "Remember that psychopath in Dallas who insisted you were his soul mate?"

"Wishful thinking," Lenny said.

"Delusional?" Trish picked up her coffee cup.

Justen made a face. "Wishful thinking, delusional, and psychopathic. We can put all of that in a song."

"Or a book." Trish's tone was harsh. "I could write a book."

She was leaning forward, her head bent. Sam put his hand on her shoulder, and she started as if his hand had hurt her. He jerked his arm back.

"I didn't mean to flinch." She looked up at him then around the table. "I haven't talked about my parents. They were addicts, and they're both dead now. I often had to stay in foster homes until they were able to prove they could take care of me." She shrugged. "It was too hard for them to stay straight, but they did the best they could. They loved me."

"Isn't that the main thing?" Justen leaned across Sam to put her hand over Trish's that were closed into a tight fist on the table.

Sam pulled back. She'd told him some of this before. He'd told her about his dyslexia. Not that it was a secret. It wasn't anything he hid and was more common in different degrees than people thought. His happened to be severe, but he figured he had consolations.

He had his music.

Now he had Callie.

"Music makes it better," he said. "That's something no one can take away."

She looked into his eyes, and he saw the yearning in them and, not thinking, drew back an inch.

Her face closed up, her eyes going hard. "I'm okay. You're right. We've got music."

"No, you're right," he said. "Sometimes it's not enough."

"Good thing you've got your librarian."

"Yeah, good thing." He dug his fork into his omelet, wanting to eat fast and go up to his room and call Callie. Make sure she was all right. And just to talk to her. Tonight. And tomorrow night, and the night after that. And every night until they were together in Nashville where he would make music, love, and wonderful memories.

And it would just be the beginning...

* * *

Mojo waited at the door for Callie. She let go of her small suitcase and knelt to pet her purring car. She kissed the furry head, then Mojo climbed onto her thighs, purring.

"You're a lot like Magic." Uncannily, a lot like Magic—except for chomping on the plant in the living room then puking it up.

But that was a small thing. A cat did what a cat had to do. Just as humans did....

Though she'd had Mojo for such a short time, she already loved her. She'd heard that cats didn't love as much as dogs, but in the short time she'd lived with Mojo, she didn't believe it. This cat, at least, loved as much as most dogs. And more than many people.

She fed Mojo then put away her clothes. Only then did she call her mom and arrange to be at her house in a half hour.

"I think I know what you want to talk about," her mom said.

She laughed, and heard the too-high pitch. "What?"

"It's like the song says. You're in love with the boy."

She opened her mouth and nothing came out.

Her mother laughed softly. "I'll see you soon. Love you."

Callie set down the phone, her heart beating fast in her ears. Her life was about to change, and she was exhilarated and scared. And wasn't sure which one was worse.

Sam had hurt her before, and as a librarian and a reader—and just a viewer of life—she knew that history often repeated itself.

How many of her girlfriends had made the same mistakes, the same bad choices, time after time?

Too many.

No one liked to think she was one of those women... But what if she was?

A meow came from the floor. She bent and scooped up Mojo, holding the small, warm cat to her chest. "No matter what, I have to find out. I have to try. I have to give it all I've got. No holding back."

She set Mojo on the floor and stood straight. "But if it doesn't work out again...it will be the last try, the last chance for him. I'll move on."

She hurried away, as if running from her words.

27

Seventeen days later

"You're here," Sam said. In the thinning, late-afternoon light, Callie stepping out of her navy blue sedan looked unreal, as if he were dreaming this.

Callie threw her arms around him, and he closed his eyes and held on to her tightly. All his doubts and worries disappeared. As if all the wrongs in the world were righted now.

Sometimes it had seemed as if he'd dreamed their night together in Chicago. And the week in Eagleton before that.

She pulled away, smiling widely at him. He beamed back, and he was only the beaming kind of guy when she was around. He wanted to do a lot more than grin at her, but not here. Her car was in the driveway, behind two SUVs and their bus, and they were exposed to the other homes on the cul-de-sac in the gated community about fifteen minutes outside of Nashville. A kid was rollerblading down the street, and Sam wasn't about to put on a show for him. Or anyone else.

Soon he would have her in the guesthouse. And he didn't plan on leaving it until the next morning.

Before he could tell her any of this, his band

members converged on them, apparently thinking three minutes was enough greeting time. From Callie's open car window came a yowl.

"Callie, I'm so glad you're here." Justen hugged Callie.

"You brought a friend." Rick nodded at the car as another yowl came out.

"A furry feline," Callie said. "Her name is Mojo, and she's not a good traveler. When I drive home, I'm going to get ear plugs."

"Mojo like the band?" Justen clapped her hands together as Callie nodded. "I love it!"

"Don't even think about going home now." Sam put his hand on the small of her back.

She glanced up at him, and her face glowed. *Love*, her expression said. *Love.*

He kept smiling at her and knew his expression was glowing with the same message.

"Welcome to Paradise," Trish said in her quiet voice. Callie turned her attention to Trish, who hugged Callie, too, but hers was more of an air hug than Justen's, their bodies and cheeks not quite touching.

Lenny hugged her, too. Though he and Trish were still sleeping together, Sam watched him carefully, his eyes narrowed. Lenny liked guitars, Harleys, beer, and football. Women came after that. A lot of women. He liked to say that he rooted for one football team, but he wasn't as fussy when it came to women.

Callie stepped back. Everyone helped carry her suitcases and the cat carrier into the guesthouse. The small kitchen was stocked, thanks to Justen and Trish. Then the others left them in what Lenny called "the love nest," gaining a narrowed-eyed glare from Trish, and Callie's cheeks flushed the same deep shade of pink as the small flowers outside their rented house. In September in Wisconsin, the flowers would be dead or would soon die. In Nashville, it still felt like summer.

Lenny was the last one out, leaving them alone in the small jewel of a house. Then she was in his arms, and he was kissing her in the way he'd wanted to kiss her outside: body to body, as close together as they could be with their clothes on. That was fine with him. Right now, he just wanted to hold her against him and savor her scent and her curves and the softness of her skin.

A loud yowl sliced into his concentration.

He stopped the kiss and lowered his forehead against hers, breathing hard.

The cat yowled again.

She laughed. "I promise you that if you ignore her, she doesn't shut up."

He groaned. "You ever wish you would've left her on Main Street?"

"Never." She stepped back. "Love me, love my cat."

He stared down at her, and her eyes were laughing at him. Love for her filled him. So much

215

love he thought it must be beaming out of his ears, eyes, and nostrils.

"Sweetheart, your cat has a new slave."

She bent to unhook the carrier door, and he headed to the kitchen. The small place had an open floor plan, and the kitchen was a dozen steps away. A noise came from behind him, a small padding sound, and he glanced around to see the black cat hurrying after him.

"You're like the Pied Piper," Callie said.

"I can play a few pipes, too."

"Really?"

She sounded impressed, and he grinned again. He wasn't a smiley kind of guy, but today he was all smiles. After the cat was fed and watered, he helped her take her suitcase to the bedroom. Once there, he closed the door behind them before the cat could follow them in.

Suitcases thudded to the floor. She laughed at him, and he whooped and pulled her close, swallowing her laugh.

In short minutes, their clothes were off, and they were on the bed. He was hungry for her. Starving. From her kisses, her laughter, and her legs wrapping around him, he could tell she felt the same deprivation. Nothing synchronized, their hands getting in the way of each other, her legs holding him close, keeping him from touching her.

But none of it stopped them. Today, enthusiasm trumped skill. And when he touched her, she was ready for him. And he was ready for her, too. He'd been ready since she'd parked in their driveway and stepped out of her Chevy.

So they made love. And the thoughts in his brain stopped, and he just *felt*. Beneath him, she made constant *ahhhs,* her fingers digging into his shoulders, clenching and unclenching.

It was hard to hold back and not to come right away, like he was a teen again. She clutched him harder, crying out, again and again, and finally he couldn't stop his release, and he shouted up at the ceiling.

Then it was done, the aftershocks shuddering through him. He lowered himself on top of her, holding her, and she held him until his shaking stopped.

He lay on her for a moment before he rolled off her. They both lay there, loose, the tension wiped out of them. Their hands moved at the same second to entwine together.

"You know what I am?" he said finally.

"The best lover on earth?"

He chuckled. "It's true, I am."

"Absolutely. But don't tell everyone. I would hate to have the women lining up outside the door, waiting for a chance at you."

"I would hate it more," he said.

She gave a funny, choking laugh.

He turned his head to look at her. She wore no makeup that he could see, and her hair was a bit scraggly, and he knew she'd driven almost straight through because of the cat, over twelve hours. Yet she was beautiful to him. She shone from the inside out, and he thought she always would.

"I'm even better than the best lover on earth," he said.

"Seriously." She raised the hand he wasn't holding to cover a huge yawn, her eyes closed. The yawn done, she opened her eyes halfway, and it looked as if it were hard to keep her eyelids up. "What could be better than that?"

"Being with you is better. I'm officially the luckiest man on earth."

She smiled, and her eyelids drifted shut. He covered her then went to the bathroom to clean up. When he returned, he thought he should eat, but he just sat there and watched her. Even when the cat crawled up to sleep with her, he watched her.

He really was the luckiest man on earth.

All they had to do was figure out how to make this last for more than three months. He was in his own Garden of Eden, and the only snake he could see in it was time.

28

"Hey." Callie opened the door for Justen to step into the living room of the guesthouse. "Is the band on break?" Callie couldn't stop the hopefulness in her voice. It was the third day, and though he'd come to her every night, her days were feeling empty.

Justen shook her head, her eyes sad, sorry for her. "Just me. The others are arguing about a bridge."

"Not the London Bridge, I suppose."

Justen blinked and opened her mouth, as if to explain, but Callie held out her hand. "That's a bad joke. I know what a musical bridge is. A different melody in the middle of the song, right? To keep the song from getting boring."

"Not exactly the way I'd explain it, but close." A meow brought Justen's attention to Mojo, who rubbed her cheek on Justen's shins. She hunkered down. "I love black cats. What a cutie." She petted her, and Mojo pushed the top of her head against Justen's palm.

"Would you like something to drink?" Callie asked, liking Justen a lot—and not just because she admired her cat, though it did help. "Coffee or tea?"

"Sweet tea, if you have any." Justen followed her

into the kitchen. "While the others argue, I thought I'd stop by and chat about places you could visit. Nashville is a terrific city, with lots to do. I envy you seeing it for the first time."

Callie handed her the glass of cold tea, resisting an urge to hug her for being so nice. It wasn't that the others weren't friendly. But their focus was on the music. They weren't here to entertain her. They were here to make an album.

"I put together a list." Callie picked up the lukewarm tea she'd left on the counter. "I'd love it if you'd look it over and tell me what I should see and what I shouldn't. This morning, I went to the local library and introduced myself to the head librarian. We're meeting for lunch later this week."

"That's cool." Justen shook her head, half smiling.

"What?" Callie asked. "You look... I don't know. Perplexed."

Shaking her head, Justen set her glass on the other side of the counter then bent over it to laugh. She finally sucked in air and straightened. "I've been in bands for too long. I'm used to bimbos, not smart librarian types."

Callie shrugged. "That's me, the rebel. Breaking stereotypes with heavy reference books."

"Or lists of museums to visit." Justen held up the list. "I wish I had time to see some of these."

"I wouldn't mind having a little less time. I might end up doing all the cooking, and I'm not the great cook my mom is."

"I'm a very good cook," Justen said, "but I only cook once in a while, or they would expect it of me all the time."

"That's what I'm afraid of." Callie sighed. "Oh well, I'm here, and it was my choice."

"And you're in love." Justen narrowed her eyes, watching her face.

Callie frowned. "Being in love doesn't mean my brains melted like vampires left out too long in the sun."

"Vampires in the sun?" Justen laughed. "Love it! You mind if I use it in one of my songs?"

"For the next album?"

"I guess we'll have to wait. Trish and I talked about collaborating on an album of girls' kickass songs, but she's not really into it." Her face expressionless, Justen flipped her long hair back over her left shoulder. "You wouldn't happen to be a closet songwriter, would you?"

"No, of course not." Callie looked out the window, feeling the heat rise in her cheeks. Mojo meowed with the same pensiveness that Callie felt inside.

"You are." Justen's voice rose. "Aren't you?"

She shook her head. "I love music, but I have the worst singing voice in the world."

"Good, because I'm the singer. I asked about writing songs."

"I don't know much about music." In school,

she'd purposely decided not to play an instrument. That was Sam's world, and she'd wanted to stay away from the boy who'd hurt her so badly.

"Writing music would be my part. I'm looking for great lyrics."

Callie took a deep breath. "In that case, I'm not the person you want. I write poetry, and it's not great. It's not even good."

"How do you know it's not good? Did you enter contests? Send to publishers? I've heard it's almost impossible to sell poetry."

Callie shook her head. "I've had two different professors eviscerate my poems. If they could have done it without getting fired, I think they would've dumped them in their wastebaskets, poured gasoline over them, and tossed in a lit match."

"Bastards."

"They were just telling the truth." The words dragged out of her. She knew good poetry. She was an English major and, at one point in her life, had read all the great poets. "One professor said it was adolescent drivel. Another said it was childish."

"But you still write?" Justen leaned forward, and her pupils sharpened. "You do, don't you?"

"I keep trying to get better." She made a face. "I feel compelled to write my little poems, but I don't let anyone else see them. Not even Sam. It's for myself."

"Love songs?"

"Sorry, no. Usually it's something I've been

going through. Or people I know. Lately I've been writing riffs on literary characters and authors." She shrugged. She wished she'd lied from the beginning, but lying was something else she was lousy at.

"Like what?"

"Scarlett O'Hara, of course. And Wuthering Heights. That kind of thing. Nothing kickass. Nothing that would fit your album."

Justen's gaze didn't waver. "I'd like to see something. And don't worry about it being terrible. Most song lyrics are simplistic. Maybe you weren't writing poetry. Maybe you were always writing song lyrics."

Callie opened her mouth to say no, then stood straight. She had the bravest mother in the world. Some days, getting out of bed when intense pain racked her body was brave. Some days smiling was brave. Telling Callie she wanted her to go to Nashville and live her own life was brave. She was the bravest person that Callie knew.

Compared to what her mother went through nearly every day, showing Justen her poems and taking the chance that Justen would smile politely and say they weren't what she was looking for was nothing.

"If you continued to write your poems after the disparagement of your professors," Justen said, her brown eyes serious, "you must love to do it. You must have a passion for it."

"It's not a passion. Just something I play around with." Her cheeks were heating again. "The majority are only a few lines. Since no one sees them but me, I don't always finish them."

"Show me," Justen said. "I'll let you know what I think."

Her hands clammy and her breaths too fast and too shallow, Callie headed to the laptop on the table. "I'll bring something up. Just don't expect a lot."

"Stop putting yourself down. I'll show you mine sometime, and you can see why I need a co-writer."

Callie sat in front of the computer, Justen at her side. Because she was nervous, Callie opened the wrong file first and had to bring up the right one. "I kind of like my Scarlett O'Hara poem, but it only has two verses."

"Let me see."

She angled her laptop toward Justen. "I don't even have a title. Here it is."

Leave the curtains, leave the home,
Don't bring a good man down low
'Cause you reap the love you sow,
If he's the right man for you,
Then Scarlett, girl, you gotta go.

'Cause Scarlett, girl, you gotta go
Go, go, go, go, go, go,
Not where the wind takes you.

You gotta go, go, go, go, go
Go where the love takes you.

Reading it, she winced, her stomach doing crunches. A third grader could write better poetry. The meter was out of whack, and it included a cliché. This was embarrassing.

Oh, well, she'd never claimed to be a great lyricist. But she made an awesome key lime pie, and the ingredients were in the guesthouse. She would make one when Justen left. That would cancel out the bad poetry. Pie had the power to cancel out the bad in most things.

Justen didn't say anything. Instead, she leaned in closer and did an odd thing. She hummed. Callie sucked in her breath shakily as Justen began to sing the words in a high, soft voice.

Callie sat back. Was Justen making music to go with her poem?

The answer came swiftly. *Yes. Yes, yes, yes.*

She put her hands to her cheeks. This was crazy. Insanity. She felt like the robot in an old TV show who kept saying, "It does not compute." She could hear Justen, but a block in her mind kept her from believing it.

Yet, in another part of her mind, she thought, *Wow, that sounds good!*

Justen turned to her. "I *love* it."

Callie put both hands over her breastbone. "You do?"

"I do!" Justen hugged her. "I might change a word or two, but those damn professors. They were probably jealous." Her phone rang. She'd left it on the counter, and went to pick it up. "Hi, honey. You won't—" She pressed her lips together, listening. "Okay, I'll be there in two minutes."

She clicked off the phone and faced Callie. "My bossy boyfriend is calling me." She closed her eyes to slits. "I'll get back at him tonight."

Callie giggled. Amazing what a few words had done to her mood. Changed her from fearful to ecstatic.

"Send me more verses. I'll look at them when I get a chance. And titles. Do you have one?"

Callie's mind clicked. "I don't always bother, but what do you think of 'Where the Love Takes you'?"

"I like it, but what about 'Scarlett's Song'? It gives me chills."

"Fine. It's great." She was so happy that if Justen told her to call it "Scarlett's Big Toe Blister," she would have said the same thing.

Callie followed her to the door. After it closed behind Justen, she peered out the window to watch Justen stride to the big house. Only when Justen stepped inside did she squeal and turn to the cat staring at her.

"Did you hear that, Mojo?" She didn't wait for a reply, though Mojo made an unhappy squawk.

As if she were warning her that there was trouble ahead.

Or else she had a hairball she was about to cough up.

Ignoring another squawk, Callie did a little victory dance.

Her life had changed. She had a lover. Not just a lover, but a man she'd loved since they were children and had thought she'd never be with. And now she had a new friend who didn't think her poems sucked, and actually wanted to use one for a song.

And her mom was still reacting well to her new treatment.

It could change soon. Change the next moment. But right now, right this minute, this second, life was wonderful.

It was like living in paradise without the poisonous snake.

The phone rang, and she sprang to answer it.

29

"Callie," a woman said, "Sam told me to call you."

Callie blinked. Who was calling her?

"We're stuck on a song."

Trish. That's who it was. Lenny's girlfriend who played the keyboard. She nodded, though Trish couldn't see her. "Yes?" There had to be more than this. But why wasn't Sam calling her?

"We're having problems. It looks like we'll be here for a while, working it out. We really like the song, but we're not sure how to fix it."

"Ah." She resisted the impulse to say, *Let me listen! Maybe I can think of something.* Right. And while she was at it, she could stop all the weird storms, punish all bullies, cure MS and cancer, and make sure politicians got along, no matter what party they were in. All of that with one wave of her invisible magic wand.

"We don't know how long it will be. I know dinner is a couple hours away, but just in case you were planning on making something, I thought it was a good idea to warn you that we'll probably be ordering pizza."

"Sounds good to me. I like pizza."

There was silence on the other end.

"Or won't I be welcome?"

"It will be a working dinner, but I'm sure Sam would be happy to have you there."

Sam? But not the rest of you? "Thank you for calling. Good-bye."

"You're not upset, are you?"

"Why should I be upset? Good-bye." She hung up. Wishing she had a land phone so she could slam it down.

She paced to the front room of the guesthouse and glared at the house across the large patio with the fire pit. She fumed. And fumed some more. Mojo jumped on the chair and stared at the house, as if she were putting a hex on it.

Her meow was plaintive. Callie petted her, and Mojo pushed her nose into her palm, and for the first time since she'd allowed Callie to house and feed her, a rough tongue licked her palm. Callie grew still, and it happened again.

Her shoulders slumped, the anger oozing out of her.

Amazing that just a few moments ago, she'd wanted to dance on the ceiling.

Now she felt more like curling into a ball on the floor.

She shouldn't be upset. After all, he was busy. She understood that. But something about the way he'd handled this, having Trish call her instead of calling himself...

She took a deep breath. It wasn't that big of a deal. She would be fine on her own.

Rubbing Mojo's neck, she bent and kissed the top of her head. "It looks like I'm going out tonight. By myself."

Her mood subdued, she sat and wrote the last two poems—still not used to calling them *lyrics*. Would they be stanzas? Or verses? She didn't even know that much.

Even with all these thoughts running through her head, her high didn't return. She was amazed that she could write with her emotions numbed down, but she was doing it. She even wrote more clearly in this darker mood. More ruthlessly. Cutting out the crap and not seeing every word as golden.

It took less than an hour. She'd been writing these bits of poetry since she was a kid and, as an adult, often did it as a kind of word game when she was home alone at night, to keep her mind busy while other women her age were falling in love and getting married and having children.

She'd been too picky to date just anyone, so instead she'd dated hardly anyone.

Now she realized she hadn't gotten over her first love. Or maybe it was that first rejection. How pathetic was that?

Very pathetic, she answered herself, her jaw firming.

When she was done, instead of obsessing over the verses as she usually did, playing with the words for hours and days, and sometimes years, she emailed them to Justen. Without pause, her emotions anesthetized, she brought up the other list, the one she hadn't shown to Justen, and studied the restaurants she'd marked down. May as well make a night of it.

One thing she wasn't going to do was stay in and mope because she wasn't with Sam.

* * *

It was still light out when the pizzas came. Callie hadn't answered the phone, and Sam had gone to the guesthouse to get her, even though the other two guys had mocked him, Rick calling him love-struck and Lenny smirking, saying he'd understand if he didn't come back for an hour or more.

Inside the guesthouse, Mojo yowled at him, though she'd let him pet her earlier in the morning.

"Sorry, sweetheart. I don't have time to play." Striding down the short hall to the bedroom, he called Callie's name. She didn't answer, and he lengthened his stride.

Their bedroom was empty. He stood just inside it, and his gut twisted. He told himself not to jump to the worst conclusion. Maybe she'd gone for a walk. Or maybe...

He headed back through the small house. Ignoring Mojo's meows, he hurried outside, closing the door firmly behind him. He gazed at the driveway, and there was one car missing. Hers.

His heartbeat slowed, and so did his breathing. Everything seemed to slow. Why would she leave without calling him or coming over? At the least, leaving him a note?

His phone was at the house, so he headed back there. The others were in the kitchen, chowing down the pizza like they were starving dogs. Lenny looked at his face first, and whatever he saw made him stop eating.

"What's wrong?"

He didn't answer, turning on his phone. He checked his messages, but none were from Callie. He found her number and called her. While it rang, he headed into the living room, away from the others.

The phone rang four times, and a robotic voice told him to leave a message. "Callie, where are you? I'm worried. Call me."

He didn't want to step back into the kitchen, but he had to find out what had happened.

"What's going on?" Rick asked. "Something wrong?"

"Callie's not there. Her car's not in the driveway." He shifted his gaze to Trish. "When you called her, what did she say to you?"

She looked surprised. "Nothing that stands out."

"What exactly did you tell her?"

"Are you accusing..." She stopped, her lower lips trembling, then visibly sucked in her breath. "I said

232

we'd hit some problems on a song and we'd be ordering pizza for dinner. That's about it."

"You sure that's all? Did she sound mad?"

"We only talked for a couple minutes. I think I even asked if it would be a problem, and she said no. I can't remember the exact words." She frowned. "I didn't know she'd get upset about it."

"Dude, you don't even know if there's a problem." Lenny put his arm around Trish's shoulder and gave her a quick hug. "Don't take it out on Trish."

Sam shoved his fingers through his hair. He was acting like an asshole. Wanting to blame someone. "I don't blame you, Trish. I—"

"Maybe you should call her yourself next time," Justen interrupted, her voice smooth.

He looked at her sharply, and she met his gaze, her expression bland.

Something icy coiled inside him. He hadn't asked Trish to call her. She'd volunteered, in case Callie was going to make a dinner for him and her.

He'd liked the idea of dinner with Callie, but this wasn't a vacation or a honeymoon. It was a time to work on the album they all hoped would take them to the next step in their career. And since it was his songs that were in the album, he had to be there. So he'd told her to go ahead and call Callie.

"She's pretty sensible," Rick said. "Maybe she went out to see a show."

"Yeah, maybe." Sam turned to Justen. "Did she

say anything to you?"

"Not about going out today, but she had a list of places she was planning to see." She cocked one eyebrow. "She's not the type to sit around and wait for you to notice her."

"I'm working."

"She knew that. It didn't seem to bother her." She flipped up one hand. "I'm just saying, she was making plans to keep busy. You can't expect her to be here at your convenience. She's not that kind of girl."

"I don't expect that." His voice came out sharper than he'd planned.

"Then what are you worried about?" Trish's voice was colored in concern, unlike the rest of them, who seemed to think it was his fault. "What did you expect?"

"I expected her to call me."

"You were working," Lenny said. "You know how you get when you're working. Like nothing else matters."

He breathed hard and shook his head. Callie always mattered. She knew that. And she was just yards away. She could've walked over and told him so he wouldn't worry. She could've left a note. It was the least she could've done.

She knew he still worried about the stalker.

"You don't think she's gone for good, do you?" Trish asked.

"She wouldn't do that." Or would she? He

pushed his hair back from his forehead. He was thinking crazy thoughts. He knew her. She wouldn't do that. And she'd left the cat. For sure she wouldn't leave Mojo.

He breathed easier, his lungs expanding.

This was small stuff, but he'd lost her twice. He didn't want to make it three times.

He wouldn't admit it to anyone else, but he admitted it to himself: He was afraid.

"Have some pizza," Trish said.

"Have a beer." Lenny held one out to him.

He transferred four pieces of pizza to a plate then grabbed the beer. "I'll wait at the house for her."

"The song!" Trish said. "What about the song?"

"Fuck the song." He reached over to the counter, grabbed another cold beer, and headed out.

As he did, another song started in his head. A drumming sound like someone running. Running, running, running. Running away from a man who didn't know why.

30

It was twilight when Callie pulled into the driveway. The guesthouse was dark, but the main house was lit up. She parked and wondered if they were still in the studio.

Her mouth tight, she picked up her purse and the shopping bag and hurried to the guesthouse. She fitted her key in the door lock, and it turned easily. Too easily. She frowned, sure she'd locked it. Most likely Sam had come in and then left again, too preoccupied with his music to realize he should lock it. Just like he was too preoccupied with his music to realize he should care about his girlfriend.

As she stepped inside, Mojo meowed and rubbed her cheek and mouth against Callie's ankle. Callie set the shopping bag and her purse on the chair by the door then bent to pet the cat.

"Hi there, sweetie. Did you miss me?"

"I don't know about her," Sam's deep voice came from the chair across the room, "but I did."

She jerked up. "Sam! You scared me."

He stood and switched on the lights. She blinked at the intensity in his dark eyes and the tightness of his mouth.

"Where were you?" His voice was sharp.

"At a book signing."

"I was worried," he said. "You could've called."

"Really?" She crossed her arms. Maybe she was overreacting, but she wasn't going to lie down and play nice. "I was under the impression that you would be working all night, and I should stay out of your way."

"That's crazy."

She raised her eyebrows, not replying.

"I didn't mean that," he said.

She stared at him, still not saying anything.

"Tell me." His voice sounded tired. "What makes you think that?"

"Trish told me the band was having a working dinner."

"No. Damn it, there must've been some kind of miscommunication."

She uncrossed her arms, holding them tight against her sides. "So, what was the message that should have been communicated to me?"

"Just that I was working, and we were going to have pizza for dinner." He pushed his hand through his hair. "*We*, meaning the band and you."

"Trish did say you'd be happy to have me there. But I definitely got the impression that I wasn't wanted."

"From now on, I'll call you myself."

"That's a very good idea."

"And if you go somewhere"—he took long strides toward her—"you can let me know."

She kept her mouth closed, because she didn't

know if she could answer him.

He put his arms around her, holding her to him. But she couldn't relax. She felt stiff.

"What's wrong?" He kissed the top of her forehead.

She pushed away from him, stepping back. "You said it was a miscommunication. In fact, the first thing you said was that I was crazy. So your first thought was that I had imagined everything." Her eyes burned, and she started past him. "And maybe you're right. I imagined you wouldn't dismiss something I said as a crazy miscommunication problem on my side."

He reached for her arm, and she jerked away. "No!" She raised her hand between them. "I'm not playing games. I'm not a person who imagines slights. But the way you said it... It just tells me that you would *prefer* not to believe me."

"That's not true."

"Then what is true, Sam?"

"That I love you."

"I love you, too, but if you're starting our relationship doubting my word..." She backed off, her hands out to hold him away. "And on something so small... I thought I took it very well. I don't expect you to always be around to entertain me. I went out and did something that I enjoyed. You're the one making a big thing out of this."

"Because I was worried." His voice was raw. "Because I didn't know where you were. Because of the stalker."

"So that gives you the right to doubt what I say?"

"No, it doesn't." He stepped closer to her, and she dropped her outstretched hands. "I was an idiot." He took another step and was so close that if he moved another inch, their bodies would be touching. "I didn't want to mess up the dynamics of the band, and you're right. Thinking you misunderstood Trish's message was taking the easy way out."

"How—"

He put his arms around her back, holding her lightly. If she wanted to step back, she could do so with ease.

But that wasn't what she wanted. She wanted to wilt against him. Tell him everything was okay, and it wasn't his fault.

She wanted to be the good girlfriend. The one who smiled and was there for him and didn't make waves.

And she was the good girlfriend. But she needed a good boyfriend, too. Someone who would trust her, listen to her. After all, she would do all of that for him.

"How do I know," she whispered, the words coming out of a dark place, "that it won't happen again?"

"Because I say so."

With a sigh, she allowed herself to lean against

him. To believe him. To trust him.

He held her tight, and a moan came out of him, like a half cry. His arms on her back, he lowered his head to the dip between her right shoulder and her neck. His arms tightened, and he held her. Nothing else, just holding her tight.

She held him tight, too. But at the back of her of mind was the thought that if he doubted her word again, maybe she wouldn't weaken the next time. Maybe she would walk away from him, and maybe she would pack up.

And maybe she would take her cat and leave.

31

Their lovemaking was hard and fierce and glorious. Then they lay on the bed on their backs, breathing hard, sweaty arm against sweaty arm. He stayed like that, not ready to break contact with her. He thought she felt the same way. He hoped she did.

He turned his head to her. Her hair was spread over the pillow, her blue eyes half open, unguarded, showing her vulnerability.

"That was good," he said.

"Best make-up sex ever." Her lips curved up.

He laughed. "You have a lot of that?"

"First time." Her smile dipped. "I wouldn't want us to be doing it too often."

"I'd be happy if it never happened again. I was apart from you for too long."

"That's the past." She twisted to her side. "I don't want our relationship to be forged out of fear and regrets. I want it to be out of love. I normally don't remember the exact words people tell me. But this time..."

He turned to his side, too. "Doesn't matter. I believe you."

She smiled brilliantly, all the lightness back, glowing straight into him.

It didn't last, his thoughts moving into darker,

heavier side roads. "I'll talk to Trish today."

"Why?"

"To let her know—"

"Know what? That what she said made me think I wasn't welcome?" She pushed up, half reclining, naked and unashamed—and desire slammed back into him. "She probably said it without thinking." She frowned. "And if I'd been more secure, it wouldn't have bothered me."

"If it's a choice between you and her..." He threaded his fingers through her hair on the side of her head, pushing it behind her ear, the silky strands sliding over the back of his hand. "There is no choice. There's only you."

"I'm not worried about Trish. I never was." She pushed off the bed, standing and facing him. "You have to work with her, so I'd prefer that you don't make a big thing about it. You said it before. If you have something to say to me in the future, you'll communicate with me directly."

"I don't want you to doubt me. I don't want you to feel insecure."

"It's not just this time." Her expression was solemn. "It happened before."

"You're talking about first grade?"

"I know we were just kids, but my heart was broken."

"So was mine." His voice thickened. "I didn't think I was good enough for you."

"But you made me feel as if I weren't good

enough for you."

He got to his feet on the other side of the bed then cursed himself and headed around the bed to her. He didn't want anything between them.

"And then I left you after the graduation party."

"I understood." But her voice was flat.

"You understood that my career was more important than you."

She shrugged one shoulder.

"So, of course when Trish said that, you weren't going to take it."

She tipped her head to the side, her expression serious. "I suspect she's a bit in love with you."

"She's sleeping with Lenny."

"But you don't think she loves him? Or he loves her?"

"Lenny's never serious about any woman. I don't know what she feels. I made it clear before you came that I wasn't interested in her. Not that way." He grimaced. This conversation was making him uncomfortable.

"So, she was into you?"

Shit, this was not going away. He rubbed the side of his face. "Maybe. I didn't sleep with her, if that's what you're wondering."

"I'm not wondering about you, I'm wondering about her."

"I've got to admit, she's not as open as the others. She had a rough childhood. Her parents were addicts. She's kind of needy, but, honey" —

one side of his lips curved up—"I never scratched that itch."

"Now I feel bad. That has to be rough, and it has to affect her as an adult."

"We all have baggage. I have my dyslexia. You have a sick mother and a selfish boyfriend."

The corners of her lips tipped up.

"And she and Lenny share a bedroom," he went on. "So she can't be that much into me."

The phone trilled, the sound coming from his pile of clothes. He took two big steps, bent down to find his cell. Looked at the name on it and turned to Callie. "It's her."

It trilled again. Callie stiffened. "Aren't you going to answer it?"

He threw it on his jeans. The phone call was bad timing. "No."

"I'll get it," she said, her tone hard with purpose, and she rounded the bed. It trilled once more as she picked it up. "Hello, Trish."

"Oh. Uh. Hi, uh, Callie. I'm glad you're back."

"I'm glad I'm back, too."

He stepped behind Callie, curving his hand over her shoulder, pressing the front of his body against the back of hers.

She glanced around at him, her eyes wide.

He grinned and slipped his hand around her front, cupping her breast. She shook her head at him, but she was smiling, so he left his hand where it was, feeling the weight and the softness as he massaged her gently.

"Trish wants to know if you're ready to work again," she said.

"I'm ready," he said, his mouth angled toward the phone. Just in case Trish had any lingering feelings for him, he wanted her to know exactly how it stood between him and Callie. And right now, things were standing very nicely. "But not for work."

Laughter came from the background of his cell, and he recognized Lenny's hooting and Justen's low, velvet laughter. He winced, realizing Trish had her phone on speaker.

Callie slapped her hand over her mouth, smothering giggles.

He took the phone from her, and she collapsed on the bed, her laughter spewing out.

The heavy load that had weighed down his heart lifted. "I'll be there in a half hour." He hung up then looked at Callie. "Are you happy now?"

Still laughing, she held out her arms. "You fool. Shut up and make love to me."

"I'm yours to command." And then he was on top of Callie, and all he could think about was that he was here with her, the woman he'd loved since they both were children, and that making love with her was the best song ever, the mix of her sighs and his, being inside her while she gasped and they touched and kissed and she gasped again, her body tightening around his.

And then his only thoughts were *yes, yes, yes,* and then, *don't come, don't come, don't come. Not yet, not yet, not yet. So good, so good, so good.*

Until finally she cried out, and her legs wrapped around him, and he couldn't stop himself, and it was wonderful and wonderful and the damn best thing that ever happened to him.

When they were apart on the bed again, he felt so much love he could have burst like an imploding sun.

He turned onto his side, the mattress giving beneath him. "Will you marry me?"

She twisted to face him. For a long moment, she stared at him—his eyes, his mouth—a small crease on her forehead. He breathed shallowly, waiting for her answer. Finally, she leaned over and kissed him, soft and tender, her lips together. Then she drew back, her eyes serious.

"I love you," he added, realizing he hadn't said it. He hadn't thought he needed to say it, because he felt it so loudly it had to be like a giant sign above his head in red, blinking lights. So how could she not know what he was feeling? But women liked being told. "I've loved you since you were four years old, and I've never stopped."

"I love you, too."

"And you'll marry me?"

"I don't know."

He nodded. "I know, I deserve that. I have to prove myself."

"Don't." Emotion shuddered in her voice. "You never have to prove yourself to me. I know what a great person you are. How smart and how talented and...and..."

"And what?"

"And how good in bed."

"Okay, that part is true."

"And talented."

He nodded. "That, too."

"And smart."

He stared at her another moment. He didn't cry. Not for years. The last time was probably when he was six, the only kid in class who couldn't read. But his eyes burned now, his throat closing up. He rolled out of bed, and he knew he should dress and leave, but he couldn't move. Just sat on the edge of the bed and worked on shoving back all the emotions he'd thought he'd buried years ago. Buried so deeply he'd never unearth them again.

But here they were, bubbling up and scorching his chest and his throat and burning his eyes.

Then she was sitting on his lap. Somehow she'd rounded the bed without him hearing her and plopped down on him. Her arms slid around his neck and shoulders, and she was still naked, and so was he.

Naked physically and emotionally. All his walls tumbled down. He didn't need them. Not with her.

He gripped her and held her tightly. Too tightly, he knew, but he couldn't seem to loosen his hold.

As if afraid that, if he did, she would jump up and go away.

And if she did that, his life would be empty.

"You're smart," she said. "Look at the music you make. The songs you write."

He laughed, only it came out as a hoarse sob, and he pushed back from her. "I'm smart." His low voice cracked. "I'm smart," he said again, louder, and this time there was only a small crack.

"You are," she said. "You're very smart."

"I'm smart." He spoke clearly this time. Fiercely. No crack, no sob. "I'm fucking smart."

She laughed wildly. "You're amazingly, wonderfully, fabulously smart."

"I am," he said, and he kissed her. Hard and fast. Then he pulled back. He didn't need anything more from her right now. The answer to his marriage question would come when it came. "Let's get dressed and go. You're coming with me."

"Is there leftover pizza?" she asked. "I've worked up an appetite."

"If there isn't, I'll order you one."

She scrambled off his lap. "I love a man who's a big spender."

He stood, too. He was a lucky man, and this time he wasn't going to do anything that would screw it up.

32

After their morning lovemaking, Callie felt too languorous to explore Nashville. She was on vacation, after all, she told the others at breakfast in the big house, ignoring Lenny's comments about it being a honeymoon time for her. Justen grinned, and Trish smiled as she played with her food, though she'd made it, taking over the food duties while the others shared cleaning chores.

Back in the guesthouse, Callie did yoga exercises, which was difficult with Mojo getting in her way then stretching in ways that she would never be able to accomplish, showing off her agility then meowing as if asking for her admiration.

After a petting session with Mojo, Callie plopped into a chair in the living room and opened up a thick book, more than four hundred pages, on Nashville's music history. When she put it down finally, she did a few more stretches after sitting for so long then picked up her netbook and logged on to her email. There was an email from Justen, who said everyone was yawning over their sweet tea, and she wanted more new lyrics.

A happy dance went on inside Callie's stomach as she pasted in part of a Jane Eyre poem she'd written:

Brooding men aren't my style
Never know what they might do
Like keep a wife locked in a tower,
And in the bedroom, they're seducing you.

Callie added: *Not a lot different between the 1800s and the 2000s. LOL Tell me if you want more.*

She pressed send, and only then did she give a squeal that made Mojo protest with a yowl. She laughed then glanced at the other emails: her mom, her dad, Sharon from the library, and a few friends. Even Brenda, Sam's mom.

She opened her mom's email first. As always, it was positive, with no mention of any pain or health problems. She tried to read the naked and uncomfortable truth between the lines to feed her guilt complex. But her mom was too smart for her, telling her about all the art shows, the concerts, and the nightclubs she and her dad had gone to.

Then her dad's email, and he only put down three lines. *I miss you. I love you. You're still Daddy's little girl.*

Closing her eyes, she imagined herself being hugged by him, and his and her mother's love surrounding her. She thought of when she was a child who was worried about her mom because she wasn't feeling well and the doctors didn't know why for a long time, and her dad would make crazy faces at her until she laughed. When her mom was having a bad day, her dad had been the one to take her to friends' birthday parties. Instead of leaving like some of the other fathers did, expecting the moms who had come with their kids to watch her, too, he'd often stay the whole time. He'd even helped her Brownie troop one year. Her mom had volunteered, wanting so badly to be part of her childhood. And she had been; she'd made it to most of the meetings, but for the ones she couldn't make, Callie's dad had taken over.

She'd hit the Great Parents Jackpot. Now she'd hit the Great Boyfriend Jackpot.

After sending love back to her dad and her mom, she opened Brenda's email. The subject line said: *Thought you'd want to know.* Callie wanted to know a lot of things, she thought, but the subject line seemed ominous, and as she clicked on it, she frowned.

Hi Callie,

Roger and I are happy that you're in Nashville with Sam. He's always been his best when he's with you—even when he was only four.

I'm trying to reach Sam. It went to voice mail, and I left a message that he should call us back, but I thought maybe I should warn you, too. I got a phone call from a blues musician last night who played at our bar when we were younger, before he moved to New Orleans. He plays piano and keyboard and gives lessons on the side. He said he gave a chick keyboard lessons a few years ago. She was already trained in the piano and wasn't bad, but she was determined to learn the keyboard. Not because her heart was pulled to it, like Sam, but because she wanted to hook up with a guy in a band.

Willy thought she was nuts, but she insisted. Only because she had some talent—and was paying cash—did he give her lessons.

She didn't tell Willy the band guy's name but let it slip that he was a drummer in a band that played a blend of blues and country. She trained with Willy for two years, and he said she was "competent" when she left.

The other night, a former band member told him that the drum-crazy kid who played while they took a break at the bar had won a Grammy. Willy looked up the song on YouTube and saw a clip of Got Mojo that someone in the audience must've put up there. He said he recognized the keyboardist as the woman he taught. Trish something. She has blond hair and it used to be brown and she's lost a few pounds, but he swears it's her.

I don't know if it means anything, but just in case she is the stalker, let Sam know.

And be careful!

Love,
Brenda

Callie read it three times. She picked up her cell phone then sat there for a long moment, because it didn't make sense calling Sam. At least now she was pretty sure that Trish had purposely tried to cause trouble between her and Sam.

With a shiver, she set the phone down. It was creepy, but it wasn't an emergency. Trish's lies hadn't split them up. When she saw Sam tonight—or earlier—she'd tell him about his mom's email.

Instead, she got off the chair and carried her laptop to the counter. She found the thick book about Nashville and set it on that, making it a better height for her to stand and type. Too much sitting wasn't good for her butt. She had stretches of just sitting at the library, but they were interspersed with periods of walking and cataloging books or other library items.

Though her job wasn't a passion and she wasn't driven to do it the way Sam and Justen were with their music, she enjoyed what she did. She enjoyed ninety-nine percent of the people she worked with. And she enjoyed ninety-nine percent of the library patrons.

But this—working on the rest of the *Jane Eyre* lyrics—was different, bringing her immense satisfaction because it was coming out of her own mind, her entire concentration focused on it. The next verse was about Heathcliff from *Wuthering Heights*, and the last verse referenced Twilight, warning the listener against men who sparkle.

She changed the title to "Brooding Men."

When she was done, she felt wiped out, dazed. It reminded her of the way she felt after sex. Not just normal sex but amazing, multiple-orgasm sex. The kind of sex that, when it was done, she just wanted to lie in bed, unmoving, and even unthinking, not letting go of that feeling of completeness and bliss.

She took a deep breath. Then read it over, and decided it wasn't anywhere near the same. Unlike orgasms, she couldn't tell if what she'd written was good or if it was crap.

A blur of movement out of her peripheral caught her attention. She glanced at the living area just in time to see Mojo land on the top of the couch and stare out the window that faced the courtyard, her back hunched, readying for an attack.

A knock came from the door, and Callie started.

Instead of hurrying to it, she remained standing by the counter, unmoving. She didn't know why. She just had a feeling that it might be better not to say anything.

"Callie?" a woman called. "Callie, are you there?"

Trish, she thought. Trish was calling her. She should step away from the counter. She should answer the door. She should—

The door pushed open. She'd thought it had been locked but then remembered there was an extra key to the guesthouse in the main house.

Callie closed the laptop, telling herself there was no reason to panic. "Yes?" she asked.

"Hi, there." Hugging a tan tote bag to her side, Trish strode toward her. "We're taking a break, and I just thought it would be nice to get to know you better."

"That's sweet of you." Maybe it was, but a chill ran up Callie's spine. Trish looked thinner than when she'd first seen her in Chicago. She'd been thin to begin with, but now she looked skeletal. And her eyes...they glittered, reminding Callie of the song she'd just written, warning young girls to stay away from men who sparkled.

They should stay away from women whose eyes glittered, too. Glittering eyes were never good.

She reached for her cell phone on the counter. "I'll call Justen to see if she'll come."

"She won't answer." Trish was marching across the dining area now. "None of them will answer. They're working on a song, and their phones are off."

Icy fear stabbed Callie's belly. She should have paid attention to her intuition that had told her something was wrong about Trish. Not just today but the other day. And she shouldn't have stopped Sam from confronting Trish. He'd had the same gut feeling that something was wrong with Trish, and she'd talked him out of acting on it.

As she watched Trish come close, horror rose in her throat. She felt frozen, the only thoughts in her mind to get out somehow. To find a weapon. To do something. Anything.

"So nice of you to stop off." Her voice was high and breathy, even she could hear it. She stepped backward, bumping into the counter. "I have some Danish. I'll get them."

"No bother. I actually bought something for you." Trish pulled a thermos out of her tote. "I know how much you like tea, and it's my special blend."

"I'm not thirsty." An image popped into her mind of the queen from Sleeping Beauty holding the poisoned apple out to Beauty.

"I'll feel really bad if you don't drink it." Trish's voice lowered, her tone a seductive timbre.

Callie shivered. "Actually, I'm a bit cold. Tea sounds wonderful. I'll get a mug."

"Good, good." Trish smiled, her lips pulled up, showing gums and teeth.

Callie rounded the island and reached up for the cup. The knives in a wooden block were close, on the other side of the sink. She glanced at them. Wondering if she could grab one. Then she heard a step and snapped around, holding the mug out before Trish could get on her side of the counter.

Her breath was coming too fast. She told herself her imagination was running wild, and Trish wasn't really going to harm her. The idea was insane.

Or else Trish was insane.

Trish bent her head, pouring tea into the mug, and Callie took a step back.

"Where are you going?" Trish asked, and her voice sharpened.

"To get you a mug, too."

The tea sloshed over the mug. Trish's breath hissed, and she set the mug on the counter then wiped her hand against the side of her top. "No need to give me a mug. I prepared this just for you. Drink it."

"I don't think—"

"You don't want to hurt my feelings, do you?" Trish's pale eyes glittered brighter, like a damn lightshow.

Callie stood straight. This was getting ridiculous. "Trish, I'm not—"

Trish's hand slid into her tote, and the tan material bulged in the shape of a gun barrel.

"A cup of tea sounds fine." Callie picked it up and her hand shook. It was filled nearly to the top of the mug, and hot liquid splashed onto the back of her hand, hurting her skin. She thought of dropping it, but then Trish pulled the tote higher, and Callie stared at the gun-barrel-sized bulge, unable to pull her gaze away.

"Drink it." Trish's voice lowered to a hypnotic whisper. "Drink it, Callie. You'll feel warm. Better.

All your troubles will float away."

She finally raised her eyes to meet Trish's crazy pale blue ones. "No," she said. Then firmer. "No."

"I'm doing this for your own sake. You don't want to feel any pain, do you?"

Callie shook her head. "Why are you doing this?"

Trish smiled and her face softened, as if she was happy at the thought of killing her. "Because you're in my way. Five years ago, Sam told me I was pretty. But he wasn't able to love me because of you. Once you're gone for good, he'll turn to me."

"You're crazy."

"Crazy in love." Her eyes glittered sharper, like broken slivers of glass, and a movement brought Callie's gaze downward, in time to watch the bulge in the tote bag crawl up.

At the same instant, a yowl sliced through the air. Callie snapped her head to the side as a black streak flew up from the table, heading straight toward Trish's head.

Mojo! Callie's heart pounded, and she watched as Trish slowly turned. Faster than a drumbeat, Mojo's underbelly slammed into Trish's face, her four legs clutching the sides of her head.

Two shrieks screamed out, one louder and sharp, the other muffled by a cat's soft belly.

Then Trish's hand whipped up in a blur, knocking Mojo off her face.

Mojo yowled. Trish screamed, turning sideways

to glare at the cat. Callie's breath sucked in. Blood oozed down Trish's face from two deep scratches. Screaming again, Trish dug into the tote and pulled out the gun. She aimed the barrel at Mojo, who was readying to jump on her again.

Without hesitation, Callie leaned over the counter and threw the hot tea at Trish's face. Trish screeched, and the gun went off, the shot a loud bang, and the bullet blasted into the wall. At the same moment, Mojo leapt at her again.

"I'll kill you!" Trish screamed, opening her eyes.

Not knowing if the crazy bitch meant her or Mojo, Callie dropped the mug, grabbed the heavy book on the counter and surged forward, sliding halfway over the smooth counter. Her breaths coming fast, she lifted the thick book up then slammed the book onto Trish's head.

Trish tottered back, the gun dropping to the floor. Her eyes wild, the glitter gone, she shrieked and dropped to the floor, too.

As Callie raced around the counter, holding the book above her head, her heart beating wildly, another scream came from Trish. Callie swooped up the gun then looked at Trish's face.

Mojo was sitting on it.

Trish lifted her arms and knocked Mojo off one more time. She peered up at Callie, who held the gun in one hand, holding the hefty reference book against her chest with the other. Then her gaze shifted to Mojo, who stood by Callie's slippered feet, as if guarding her.

Whimpering, Trish covered her face with her hands. "Keep the cat away from me. Keep it away!"

Callie didn't answer her. She set the book on the counter and, holding the gun with one shaking hand, she turned on her cell and called nine-one-one.

"Sam," she said. "Is Sam alive?"

But Trish just sobbed into her hands, and on her cell phone, a woman's voice said, "Nine-one-one."

33

The nightmare continued with the police finding Sam and the other band members unconscious in the house. The gray-haired detective told her the EMT said their heartbeat and breathing seemed to be slow but okay. They seemed to be in a deep sleep.

"Like Sleeping Beauty," Callie said, hearing the high pitch of her voice.

He laughed then cut it off, his forehead furrowing.

"When she tried to make me drink her tea," Callie continued, "she reminded me of the wicked queen in Sleeping Beauty."

"Yeah, well, the wicked queen didn't get away with it, and thanks to you, neither did Ms. Wellington."

It took a couple seconds for Callie to connect *Ms. Wellington* with *Trish*.

She could hear the ambulance siren as it sped away from the house. She twisted to face the direction it was moving in. "I want to go to the hospital with them."

"They'll probably be out for a while. We'd like to talk to you a bit, and then you can go."

She wanted to fall apart, to scream at him, tell him she *needed* to be with Sam. Instead, she reminded herself of all that her mother had gone through without falling apart. And all that her father had gone through, too. Yet they always remained strong.

So she answered the questions put to her by the detective and his partner, a Hispanic male not much taller than her. When they told her how brave she'd been to do it all alone, she shook her head. "I wasn't alone. I had my cat."

They glanced around, and on cue—as if she'd heard what they said and had been waiting to take her bows—Mojo popped up on top of the sofa back. Of course, she hadn't understood what they'd said, Callie thought. Then Mojo meowed, as if to say, *Yes, I am the true hero.*

The two cops laughed, and a shiver ran through Callie.

This was a very odd day.

* * *

Slowly, moving carefully, Sam pushed up and rotated until he sat on the side of the hospital bed.

"You feel good enough to get out of bed?" the detective asked, a big man who looked as if he could've been a football player at one time.

"I feel like something scraped off the bottom of a farmer's boot."

"I've felt like that a few days," the detective said.

The female detective snorted, a scornful sound.

"I had a ten-pound-eight-ounce baby during a blizzard with no painkiller."

Sam winced, and the other detective groaned as he handed Sam a shoe. "You don't know how often I've heard that story."

"We're not here to talk about us," the female detective said, a tall, broad-shouldered woman with short, tight curls. They'd both introduced themselves to Sam when they'd come in, about a half hour ago, but his mind had been fuzzy then

"If it's any consolation," the male detective said to Sam, "you were never intended to be a victim. You were supposed to wake up and not know anything until you found your girlfriend's body."

Sam stopped putting on his shoe and glared at the detective. "You think finding my girlfriend dead instead of me is a consolation? Looks to me like that's a wedding band on your left hand. I feel damn sorry for your wife."

His female partner gave Sam an approving glance. "I've had that same thought a thousand times. But you can't go. The doctor hasn't signed a release."

"Then let the doctor pay for my overnight stay, because I can't afford it." Just talking hurt his head and his belly, but he had a burning need to get out of here and see—

"Sam." His softly spoken name cut straight to his heart like a pure note on a guitar. His head snapped up as Callie stepped into the hospital room with the gray-blue walls, her eyes on him, as if only he mattered.

He dropped the shoe and stood, holding back the nausea and the dizziness, his arms out. She walked into his arms, and he still felt like crap...but he also felt like the luckiest man in the world.

He leaned his head on hers. "I'm sorry," he whispered. "You were almost killed because of me. I'm sorry."

She pulled back above her waist, their thighs still touching. "Don't you dare take any blame for what that woman did. You didn't ask for it. You didn't see inside her brain."

"Yeah, but I..." He stopped. "You're right."

"I know. I'm always right." She smiled, and it was as if a hundred suns shone brightly. "You can remember that."

"For the rest of our lives."

He bent to kiss her. From the door came the sound of someone entering the room, then the cops were yelling at someone to get out of there. Then yelling that he needed to leave the camera. Then came the sound of running feet.

But Sam didn't lift his head, and neither did she. Both of them hung on tightly to each other.

In the middle of this messy life, he had the feeling he'd be hanging on to her for as many years as they lived.

34

Seven months later

"Congratulations to the two newlyweds! Aww, you're blushing. That's so cute." The too-thin interviewer aimed a question at Callie, even though Callie sat farthest from her on the end of the sofa. She and Sam were still in the rental house while they were redoing the house they'd bought, and the interviewer had come to them rather than the other way around.

The interviewer's chair was kitty-corner from them, the chair and sofa arranged to form an uneven V, with Rick and Justen closest to her, Lenny in the middle, then Sam and her at the other end. Callie had thought she'd be safe so far away, but after all that had happened recently, she should have known there was no safe place in life.

Sam's manager had begged Callie to be a part of the interview. The band's new album was out now, released last week.

So of course, she'd said yes to the interview. It was business. Publicity. Besides, she'd survived an attempt on her life by a crazy woman. She'd survived the paparazzi who'd snuck in while they were in the hospital. She would survive this, too. Anytime she was asked a question, she reminded herself she was doing this for the band's future.

Rick had said that the Grammy had given them credibility, but the psycho chick had made them famous.

The interviewer asked the members about the songs first then aimed her gaze on Justen's face. "I heard you're making your own album."

Justen smiled with her mouth closed, looking cool and amused. "It's not my own. The lyrics were mostly Callie's. The music was mine."

"You're putting this out yourself?"

Justen shook her head, smiling calmly at the interviewer. Callie admired her so much. She was so confident, like a goddess. An earthy goddess. From Callie's knowledge of the classics, most of the goddesses were earthy and passionate.

"I could've put it out by myself, but I'm happier doing it with these wonderful musicians." She smiled at Rick, holding his hand. "And a very sexy singer."

He grinned at her, but the interviewer's next question made his smile turn sour.

"Did this have anything to do with the near death?"

Callie stiffened. She'd known this was coming, but still she wasn't ready for it. The interviewer had been softening them up. Like someone taking a steak and pounding it to tenderize it.

But Justen's smile didn't dip. Callie saw that, unlike her, she hadn't allowed herself to be tenderized.

"What happened with Trish did affect us," she said. "It drew us together. We were strong before, and going through this together made us stronger."

"Separate, we're good." Rick put his hand on her shoulder, claiming her. "Together, we're amazing."

Justen nodded. "We make each other better."

"What about you?" The interviewer switched her gaze to Callie. Leaning forward, she showed some upper boobage. "I hope I'm not making you uncomfortable. Or scaring you."

"I fought off a woman who wanted to kill me." Callie clipped the words out. "You certainly don't scare me."

A choked sound came from one of the crew, but the interviewer smiled so brightly it had to be fake. "You are plucky."

"I'm a librarian. We're a plucky breed."

The interviewer grinned, a real smile. "I spent hours at the library when I was a child. I love librarians. But you're more than a librarian now. And more than a wife."

"Justen and I co-wrote the lyrics, but I couldn't have done it without her. And I hope that all women are more than one thing. And all men, too." She looked up at Sam. "I'm married to a genius."

He squeezed her hand, and looking into his eyes, she saw the glow in them.

"Yes, but you were the one to save him," the interviewer said. "You're a heroine."

"He wasn't in any danger." Lenny frowned. He'd matured since the day Trish had drugged them and tried to kill Callie.

"You were." The interviewer stared at Callie. "How do you feel about that?"

Her heart pounded, and she took a calming breath before replying. "Lucky to be alive."

The interviewer laughed. "You're good. Very good."

"She's fantastic." His arm around her shoulder, Sam gave her a quick squeeze.

"Trish's sentence was just ten years." The interviewer voice was gentle and sympathetic, but her eyes were obsidian, giving Callie shivers. "The charge was reduced to aggravated assault. She got off easy. There was a lot of anger over this on social media. Your fans were furious with the justice system. What do you think about it?"

Callie's body tensed. She put her hand on Sam's thigh near his knee, giving him a cautionary squeeze so he wouldn't say anything he'd regret.

"I think she's given up ten years of her life," he said. "She'll be in her late-thirties when she's out. She's talented, and I hope she rebuilds her life." His voice was rough, and he squeezed Callie's shoulder again. "She tried to kill Callie, and it didn't work. We have everything now, and she has nothing. I hope she gets help."

The interviewer's face softened. "You're so sweet and forgiving." Her eyelids lowered, her voice purring. "And very handsome. I can see why she fell in love with you." She turned her gaze back to Callie. "As much as you deny it, you're the real heroine of the day. If you hadn't stopped her, you'd be dead. And though she fancied herself in love with Sam, if he'd come to, and she didn't like his reaction, she might..." She made a slicing motion with her index finger over her neck, her mouth in a grimace.

"Honest," Callie said, "the heroine wasn't me. No one seems to believe me, but the real heroine is right there." She pointed at the carpet-lined climbing ladder, about five-feet tall, that her parents had brought with them from Eagleton when they'd driven up for their wedding. Mojo was sitting on the top perch, her chin up, as if she were posing for the camera.

"She's gorgeous," the interviewer said.

"And smart." Sam squeezed Callie's hand. "All the women in my life are smart."

There was general laughter, and Justen called out, "Thanks, Sam!"

The interviewer was smiling widely, another real smile compared to the one that hadn't reached her eyes when she'd begun the interview. "I wonder what the cat would say if she could talk."

"You don't know that cat," Rick said. "She talks all the time. I'm sure she's trying to say something to me."

"What do you think she's trying to say?"

"That she's smarter than him," Justen said.

"Than all of us," Rick replied.

"She probably is," Justen said.

"I have to agree with Sam." Callie bent toward the cat. "Mojo, are you trying to talk to the pretty lady? Don't be shy. What's the message you'd like to give to her?"

Mojo yowled, and the interviewer gave an *eep,* not expecting it.

As if she choreographed her next move, Mojo lifted a back leg straight up in the air then lowered her head and craned it so she could lick her butt.

While the others laughed, including the film crew, Sam bent down to kiss Callie quickly.

Smiling, she leaned against him. Right now, if she had to sit down and write a song, she knew what the title would be. "Life Is Good."

In fact, right now, life was amazing.

35

The strangers left, and shortly after that, so did the others. Now it was just the two humans and Mojo.

Mojo ate the food that they'd given her. Human food. Sam said she deserved the good stuff, and of course, she did.

With that kind of talk, Mojo didn't mind sharing Callie with him.

After all, the food she was eating now was much better than when she'd been a dog.

The humans went to bed. Not to mate again— they'd done that earlier. This time was to sleep.

She entered the bedroom and remained still, listening for sounds that might be mice or other animals.

When she was certain that any rodents in the area had gotten the message that she was here, and if they valued their lives, they should stay far away, she jumped onto the bed and curled up on a spot between their legs. Once she was comfortable, she thought about the extraordinary changes that had happened to her.

The humans thought this was all about them, but that was humans for you.

In truth, it was all about her.

The real heroine of the story.

It had taken some time to figure it out. Bits of memory had come to her during her days with Callie. The most important part had returned in the kitchen, with the woman who'd oozed a smell that made Mojo think of death.

She knew about death.

It had happened to her.

She didn't remember the details, but she had been a dog. A male dog. He had loved Callie, and Callie had loved him. Every day when Callie had been at school, he'd waited for her to come. And when she hadn't come home—when she'd stayed after school for any reason or visited with a friend—he'd sat by the door and waited until she came home.

At night, when Callie went to bed, the dog had jumped up on Callie's bed and slept with her.

When he'd gotten old and his legs had hurt and his muscles had weakened, he hadn't been able to jump on her bed.

So Callie had pulled her pillow and cover to the bedroom floor and slept with him.

And then he'd been taken away from Callie, and he hadn't been ready. Hadn't been nearly ready.

Callie had needed him.

But it hadn't mattered. He'd been taken away from her anyway.

Mojo didn't know who *they* were. The ones that had control over her.

Her mind was blurry on that part.

272

All she knew was that she had come back for Callie. Come back when Callie needed her. Come back to save her.

Come back so she would be happy.

In return for saving Callie, all Callie and Sam had to do was love her and feed her for the rest of her life.

Her eyes closed, she curled up tighter to sleep.

She knew about books from Callie, and to her, it felt like one book was over...and another book was just about to begin....

About Edie Ramer

Edie is funnier on the page than in real life. A *USA Today* bestselling author, she lives in southeastern Wisconsin with her husband and one important cat.

In addition to her Rescued Hearts and Miracle Interrupted series, she's published in paranormal and sci fi romance, plus a humorous mystery. She's happy to be able to do what she loves nearly every day.

Stay updated on all of her releases and special sales by subscribing to her newsletter:
www.edieramer.com/newsletter/